CLAIMED BY THE PACK

A REVERSE HAREM PARANORMAL ROMANCE

JADE ALTERS

RIDGE

"Courtney will skin you alive, Ridge."

I rolled my eyes at my always worried friend, Chase. We called him Chase because all he did most days was chase his own tail. Courtney, our female alpha and the leader of our pack, took pity on him when she took him in, I think.

He's a nice guy and if we hadn't taken him in, he'd be alone on an island and in constant danger from other, established packs. Normally the male and female alphas would chase away a lone wolf, maybe even kill him.

But our pack was different. It was started by Courtney and her four mates.

Yes, I said four.

I know it's slightly unorthodox, but it works for us. The fact that our alphas all five spent most of their lives as strictly human was probably the most unorthodox part of it all, but like I said, it works.

The pack was formed in the deserts of Afghanistan and the five of them, along with their pup, traveled to Bali, looking for a place to start over. Along the way they've collected strays, myself being one of them.

We were about 20 strong, mostly males, pups and old women. As my name might imply, I was found wandering along a ridge on Komodo Island.

My family was killed, except for me and a younger pup named Grayson who I'd been told to protect.

Grayson was the son of the alpha and it was important to the pack he survive. I'm a beta, but was one of the strongest of our pack, so that's how I ended up with the assignment.

I don't necessarily blame the humans. We had a renegade omega in our pack. He was killing farm animals then humans. Before he could be dealt with, the humans came for all of us. They didn't know what we were, they just believed they were dealing with an overpopulation of wolves.

Courtney and her mates found Grayson and me and invited us in, with open arms. Since then, we've both learned a lot about being human as well as being a wolf. Our pack lived mostly in our fur and sometimes we were hungry and cold.

Since we joined up with Courtney's pack, our bellies have always been full, we've slept warm and dry at night and we lived more as human than wolf, which I was getting used to.

My only complaint was the lack of females in our pack. Courtney had no objection to us finding a human mate, but she wanted us to do it the old-fashioned way. I'm 23. I need a mate, and I hate to say it, but I don't see anything wrong with the way my kind has done it for God knows how long.

"I'm not going to hurt her," I told Chase. "I'd never hurt a woman."

"You're just going to drug her a little bit."

"You know how much respect I have for Courtney and her mates, but they all lived most of their lives as humans. She doesn't understand the old ways. She's coming around to a few of them..."

"But, she specifically forbade us from using the drug for mating."

"I'm done curling up alone at night, Chase. I'll take the consequences. I'll handle it. I want this woman and she won't give me the time of day."

"Maybe that means she's not interested."

"She's afraid. She's had a bad go of it with men. I'll show her a whole new world."

"And that's what concerns the pack. You show her our world and she tells everyone else and then we're exterminated the way your pack was, and mine."

Chase was found on the island of Bali where the pack had intended on settling. He'd come from a very small pack. Some of them died off from hunger or old age, but the majority of them had been hunted. Chase was a pup when he lost the last of his pack. He barely survived, high up in the woods, alone.

Like me, he knew little to nothing about functioning as a human. The pack found him and took him in.

He's got a lot to learn, but his heart is in the right place.

Bali was where the pack intended to settle, originally, but they found it to be too overpopulated, mostly thanks to all of the tourists.

THE PACK MOVED onto Komodo Island from Bali and finally settled on an island just north of Komodo. It's unincorporated and many people don't know about it. The population was under a thousand, counting us. There were plenty of places for us to run, and hunt and frolic in the woods without drawing attention.

We blended in with humans easily most of the time, but keeping us in our human skin too long is like keeping us in a cage. The locals call the island "Surga" which in Indonesia means, "Paradise," and I would agree that it was, if not for the lack of females.

My main problem with doing things the old-fashioned way as a human was that it took so much time. You couldn't just spring who and what you were on them without running for the hills, or the cops.

In my world we mated with another wolf, or we used the drug for humans. By the time they woke up, they were one of us. Sometimes it was slightly traumatic for them, but I've never seen one that didn't come around...eventually.

I wanted to do it the way my parents had done it, and their parents, and my great grandparents before them, but the youngest female wolf in our pack was Courtney, and she was certainly taken. Then, the next youngest was in her 50's. I loved her like a mother, but definitely not a mate.

"There she is," I told Chase.

My eyes were drawn to her whenever she was in the room. Her name was Cheyenne and she's beautiful. She's from the US, Native American, she told me, in case I couldn't guess. She had that look about her.

The high cheekbones, long, shiny dark hair and big, round dark eyes gave it away. Her eyelashes were so long that at first you might think they're fake, but they're not.

WHAT I LIKED MOST WAS that her body wasn't rail thin like a lot of human girls. When I first saw her, I noticed that she had curves...so many curves, curves my palms itched to explore.

I could tell the few times I talked to her that she was somewhat insecure, probably because the curvy girls in Indonesia are few and far between.

Her two friends that came out with her every week are rail thin. One of them looks Indonesian and the other was a blonde, probably also from America. They're both beautiful women...but not like my Cheyenne. She was the one I wanted.

5

CHEYENNE

nother Friday night out in Surga. I both loved and hated my new life. Just before I graduated from college with a BA degree in finance and a minor in mathematics, I was offered an opportunity that I couldn't pass up. My father's best friend lived in Indonesia and had houses in both Bali and on this small island called Surga.

Surga was an unchartered island, found by a group of fishermen in the late 90's. The story goes that it was bought by a billionaire who built homes there for the poor and needy who roamed the streets of Bali. He built an entire little town for them, a haven, so to speak. When he died, he left the island to one of its inhabitants with the stipulation that it couldn't be sold, only passed on to whomever he chose to be his heir.

The guy was about 50 years old now and he owned the bar I had just walked into. He was a super nice guy, and a lot of fun, but mostly everyone hung on his every word and every crazy story in the hopes of someday becoming his heir.

Meanwhile the population of the island continued to grow. It was a collection of people who simply wanted to live off the grid, people hiding out from one thing or another and people like me, here for work.

My boss was a contractor and owned a real estate business. He dominated the market on Surga and his men were always busy.

I did the payroll, taxes and other administrative tasks. It was a good job and my boss was generous with my wages and benefits. The island was gorgeous. I couldn't have dreamed up a more beautiful place to live. But at 21 years old, with a chubby build and shy personality, being on an island of 650 people, where the median age is 42...well, it can get a little lonely sometimes.

My two girlfriends and I had a standing date every Friday night for drinks and dancing at a local club called "Park's Place". Park was the last name of the guy who owned the club and it was always a fun time.

My roommate Marta and our co-worker Bonnie were my best friends. They're both slim, beautiful and outgoing and were constantly surrounded by men.

I get hit on sometimes too...usually by a sailor who's been out to sea for too long, or one of the old, married men, looking for a little fling.

I wasn't interested in either.

I promised myself that no matter how lonely I got, I wasn't going to settle. I've spent the past six months on this island, not settling, and not dating. But a few weeks ago, I'd met a man at the club who I couldn't get off my mind. He was in the bar tonight.

I saw him as soon as I walked in. Of course, I was looking for him. Something about him, beyond the fact that he was drop-dead gorgeous, drew me. He introduced himself to me one night and tried to buy me a drink.

I turned the drink down.

Although I hadn't been given any reason to worry on the

island, I was still wary of someone slipping something in my drink. It had happened to a close friend of mine in college back in the states. She was raped and never the same afterwards.

He told me he understood, and asked if he could sit with me and talk. There were so many beautiful women in the place, I was confused and maybe a little suspicious about why he'd picked me. He did most of the talking, but I have to admit that he was really good at getting me to open up, more than I would usually to a stranger.

The night ended however, without him asking for a date, or even my number. I was disappointed, but not necessarily surprised.

Oh well..

I saw him one other time and we had just started talking when a man came in the bar. A big, burly man with a beard. He was nice looking too...but kind of scary and dark.

He came up and said something in Ridge's ear and then walked away, like I wasn't even there. Ridge was profusely apologetic and said he had to leave, and he hoped we could meet up again...but still, he didn't ask for my number or a date.

Maybe he had a hot girl at home and I was just for conversation. It happened to me all the time. I was a good listener and even in high school, no real threat to the girls the hot guys actually dated.

They came to me when they needed to talk, and the hot girls got them the rest of the time.

"I'm going to get us some drinks," my friend Marta said into my ear. "Grab that table over there in the corner, okay?'

"Sure," I yelled back.

Bonnie already saw a guy she knew and was huddled close to him, talking. I knew she liked him, but when she first met him he had been in a relationship.

He recently broke up with the girlfriend and Bonnie was slowly but surely moving in for the kill. She was blonde, green-eyed and a fashionista. I had no doubt she'd soon be dragging him around on her arm, with him practically begging to do her bidding.

I made my way over to the table in the corner, stealing glances in the direction of Ridge...even his name was cool.

Too cool for me.

I shook off the thoughts in my head and sat down at the high-top table. Forcing myself to focus on anything else, I looked out at the dance floor, watching all the people hugging each other, rubbing up against each other, kissing and swaying to the music.

A pang of jealousy and loneliness assaulted me just as I heard a deep, baritone, melodious voice say,

"Well there she is, hello Cheyenne. It's so good to see you."

I turned to look at him.

"So good" didn't even describe the way that seeing him made me feel. Strangely, although I knew very little about him, that pull was ever-present. I'd never felt anything like it before and it confused me.

"Hi Ridge. How are you?" He slid a long leg over one of the tall stools and then he touched me...for the first time. He slipped his hand under mine and the contact was electric. I was staring into his beautiful hazel eyes, but it was hard not to look down.

My whole arm was tingling.

He smiled and a part of me melted as he said, "Just fine, now."

The spell was broken by the sound of Cheyenne's friend's voice.

"Here you go," she said, "One Cosmopolitan. Hi Ridge."

Cheyenne introduced her friends to me the first night we met. They seemed like nice enough girls but I preferred having her to myself.

Growing up mostly in the woods, as a wolf, I didn't have a lot of experience being around groups of women.

They tended to whisper and giggle too much for my taste. I was a very direct guy and all that whispering and giggling kind of annoyed me. I felt like if you had something to say, you should just say it.

If it were simply up to me, and I thought it wouldn't freak her out, I would tell Cheyenne how I felt and then I'd take her to the woods, and change her.

I could feel her vibes. I knew she was having feelings for me, but in typical human fashion, she was fighting them.

"Hello Marta," I said, politely, while hoping she'd go away. "So nice to see you again."

"You too," she said. She whispered something into Cheyenne's ear and they both giggled.

Then Cheyenne said,"Go on. I'm okay."

To me she said, "So are you here with your friend Chase again tonight?" I'd introduced Chase to Cheyenne the first night I met her.

Something about the vibe between them made me change my mind about having him around when I talked to her though. Their vibe wasn't nowhere near as strong as mine and hers...but, it was there and I didn't like it.

I respected my alphas and their ability to share Courtney, but I didn't like sharing. When I get Cheyenne to believe she's my mate, I'm not going to share her with anyone.

"Yes," I said. "He's on the prowl out there somewhere."

Poor Chase didn't have much luck with women. He was a good-looking guy, I guess, but he had no idea how to talk to a woman. I was just winging it myself most of the time, but it seemed to work for me a lot more often than it did him.

Cheyenne's eyes scanned the crowd on the dance floor and I felt a tickle of jealousy, thinking she was looking for him. The sudden loud burst of laughter from a table behind us prompted her to smile herself and say, "Hopefully he's careful. It sounds like the hyenas are out in full force."

I laughed. I loved that she had a sense of humor and that she was just so real, and I told her so.

"You're not just another pretty face. You're witty too."

I watched the color rise in her cheeks.

"Sure, whatever you say," she said, picking up her drink and hiding her face behind it for several seconds. I watched her eyes scan my face. It was like she was always trying to figure out what I was thinking...or why I was with her.

I couldn't figure out how she didn't know how incredibly beautiful, and sexy she was. When I made her mine, I would spend the rest of our lives proving it to her.

"So there's a question I've been wanting to ask you, Cheyenne. Why don't you have a boyfriend? You're much too wonderful to be alone."

Another blush and then a slight roll of her eyes like she thought I was simply using my lines on her. "I haven't had the best of luck with relationships," she said, leaving it at that.

"Hmm, sounds like you've been looking for long-term in temporary people. Some men have no idea how lucky they are to have a beautiful, sexy, funny, smart woman, until it's too late."

Her blush grew darker and she said, "You don't have to say things like that. I'm happy to just sit and talk to you, about real things."

I raised an eyebrow and said, "All I ever talk about are real things. You, Cheyenne, are the realest thing I see in this club and I meant every word I just said."

She fidgeted with a straw with both of her hands and looked away when she said, "You could have any woman you want in this club...any woman on the island. You can't expect me to believe that you look around this room and see all these gorgeous women and truly believe that I'm the most beautiful."

I reached over and put my fingers underneath her chin and tipped her face up so she would be forced to look at me. "I do expect you to believe it, Cheyenne, because it's true. Take a walk with me, Cheyenne, in the moonlight. Let's get out of this stuffy place and get some fresh air."

Her eyes widened and I saw her scan the room for her friends. This was the part about the old-fashioned way, that annoyed me. I was too impatient to wait until she began to believe I genuinely had feelings for her, and she ran it by her friends and her family.

I wanted her...right now. "Um...I'm not sure that's such a good idea."

I covered her hand with mine, stopping the fidgeting, and looked into her eyes and said, "Cheyenne, you don't think I'm going to hurt you, do you? I would never hurt a woman, especially not you. You'd be safer with me than anywhere in the world, I guarantee you that. Did I tell you that I work for The Pack?"

The Pack was the name of our security company, and it was quickly gaining a sterling reputation on the island. We didn't have a police force of our own. They had to come over from Bali or Komodo and sometimes that took too long.

The citizens had begun to turn to us for many of their safety needs. The alphas, Courtney's mates, had begun installing security cameras in some of the darker places in town where crime had increased in recent years. So far in the short time we'd been there, our pack had been responsible for the apprehension of over a dozen criminals who had been terrorizing the locals for a long time before we even got there.

I could tell by the look on Cheyenne's face that she knew exactly who The Pack was.

"Your company does a lot of business with the company I work for," she said. "My boss used to have a company come over from Bali to install the security systems on the new properties he built, but he's been using your company almost exclusively for months now."

"Awesome," I told her with a wink. "So see, there's a connection between us that should make you feel more comfortable with me."

She smiled. "And...that could be just your angle...getting me to feel comfortable with you and let down my guard."

I laughed. "I guess you could be right, but you're not. I just want to get to know you, Cheyenne. I want to spend some real time with you."

"Then maybe," she said, still not looking like she believed

me, "Maybe we could go on a date or something." I resisted the sigh I felt inside. Dates were fine and once she was my mate I'd take her on as many dates as she wanted to go on.

But, no matter how pissed Courtney and the alphas were going to be with me...I had to have her sooner, rather than later.

"Okay," I said, pretending to be placated with that. "We'll go on a date." I wasn't lying exactly, we would, eventually go on many dates. "At least let me buy you a fresh drink," I said, looking at her almost empty glass.

She'd never let me buy her a drink before, but I hoped she was finally comfortable enough with me that she would tonight. She looked at the glass like she was contemplating it and then at last she said, "Okay, sure. I'd like another. I'm driving tonight though, so that'll be my last for the night."

"Perfect," I told her. "I'll be right back." I made my way through the crowd and to the bar. I asked the bartender for a beer and a Cosmopolitan when I felt someone standing way too close.

I turned, almost ready to fight, and came face to face with Chase. "Damn it, Chase. Don't sneak up like that."

"Feeling guilty about something?"

"I don't feel guilty a bit. She wants me too."

"Don't do this, Ridge." Poor Chase worried all the time, about everything. I didn't know if he'd always been that way, or if his time alone on that island, always looking over his shoulder had done it.

Sometimes I thought he could use a good dose of something just to calm him down.

"It'll be fine," I said, picking up both drinks. I had the pill in my right hand and as I pulled the glass off the bar, I squeezed it, forcing the drug out through the tiny little hole I'd made with a safety pin.

It wasn't anything that would hurt her. It would simply

make her sleep until I could get her into the woods, and she and I could spend enough time alone for her to realize I was her mate and agree to becoming one of us. I was confident that she would and Chase was worrying for nothing. "Go enjoy yourself," I told him.

"And when I get back to the compound what should I tell the alphas about where you are?"

"If they ask, and it's unlikely that they will, just tell them I met a girl. It's not a lie."

"Ridge..."

"Beat it, Chase. I mean it. Don't screw this up for me." I left him standing there and headed back over toward my beautiful mate, drinks in hand...ready to begin our life together.

I couldn't believe that he finally asked me out...well, sort of.

He said we could go on a date, but he didn't say when or where. Maybe he was still just messing with me, still trying to get me to agree to leave with him, thinking he was going to get an easy piece of ass. I can't deny that those feelings were raging inside of me. I wanted him...who wouldn't.

He's hot, he's funny, he says all the right things. But I wasn't willing to sacrifice all I had gained in the past year, and by that I meant the confidence that my last boyfriend I had taken away.

He stripped it day by day...slowly chipping off a piece every day until I was left believing I was everything he said I was, and what he said I wasn't. He told me I was fat, unattractive, dumb...all the things that Ridge was telling me just the opposite about.

But my old boyfriend had said all the right things in the beginning too, and he wasn't half as hot as Ridge. Where my ex could have had half the women in this room, Ridge could have had all of them if he wanted to, and then some.

"Here we go."

Ridge sat the drink down in front of me. I automatically looked into it. I'm not sure what I thought I'd be able to see...pills floating in it or something crazy obvious. I smiled at Ridge and said, "Thank you."

"My pleasure," he said, sitting back down on the stool next to me and picking up his beer. He held it up and said, "To us spending much more time together...soon." I assumed he was talking about the "date," but thought that was a vague way of putting it.

My suspicious mind was working overtime. I picked up my glass and said, "To getting to know each other." He smiled and gave me a little nod before tapping his mug to my glass and taking a long drink of his beer. I did the same with my drink, noting that it tasted exactly the same as the last one, and I was entirely silly for worrying.

"So, how did you get into the security business?" I asked him.

"Well, I've always thought about becoming a police officer...but, I'll be honest with you, I'm not the most patient man in the world. The police academy is nine months long and I didn't want to wait nine months. I needed a job, but I like immediate gratification."

"So you got a security job?"

"Yes, but not just any security job. The Pack is run by a group of men who are ex-military special forces. They were willing to train me, and in the year that I've been with them, I've probably learned twice or even three times as much as I would have in the police academy."

"Well that's..." a sudden wave of dizziness almost knocked me off my stool. My head spun so hard that I actually put both of my hands on the table in front of me and held on tightly.

"Cheyenne? Are you okay?" I looked at Ridge and realized

my vision was weird too. I could see him, but nothing else around him. It was like his beautiful face was at the center of a clear prism.

He was framed by a blur of lights and color. "Cheyenne?" He said my name again and I heard it, but inside my head, not through my ears. All that I could hear in my ears was the relentless pounding of the blood flowing from my head to my rapidly beating heart.

"I-I'm not feeling so good," I said, as the dizziness and the other weird stuff was joined by a bout of nausea. I saw Ridge come out of his seat and felt his arm go around me.

"Let's get you some air." He was sliding me off my stool and into his arms. I felt like I was going to vomit all over him and I panicked.

"No Ridge...I'm okay..." The edges of my vision changed again, and everything was gray. I could still see his face, but the gray fog that surrounded it blurred his features. I felt my legs giving out. I couldn't stand on them...but then I realized they hadn't given out, Ridge was holding me around my waist, and up off the floor about an inch, and he was carrying me through the crowd toward the back door.

Once again, I panicked as he pushed through it and took me with him. I felt the rush of cool ocean air and I couldn't hold back the vomit any longer. I doubled over, emptied my stomach and I felt myself begin to cry. I couldn't stop. I was shaking all over and I realized that Ridge was stroking my hair and telling me everything would be okay. I thought he was so sweet, to stick by me the way he was. And then just as everything around me was fading to black I heard him say,

"You'll sleep it off quickly, and the rest of the night will be ours."

CHASE

"What do you mean, you don't know where he is? Chase, you know the rules. Our hard and fast rule is that no one disappears without telling someone where they are, where we can find them."

"I know, I'm sorry. Did you try calling him?"

Courtney frowned at me. "Of course I called him. I've called him a dozen times over the past two days. And you want to know something, Chase?"

"What's that?"

"I would be really worried about him...but since you're our resident worrier, and you don't seem to be worried about him at all..."

"I'm worried," I told her. "Look," I held up my hand. "It's shaking."

Courtney looked like she wanted to smile, but she didn't. She kept the stern look on her face and said, "I see that, but you see Chase, I believe you're worried...about yourself. You're worried about how mad I'm going to be when I find out you're covering for him. It's not like Ridge to disappear, so either something happened to him, or he's up to something that he shouldn't be. Which is it, Chase? Talk to me."

I reached up and wiped the sweat off my brow. The rest of the pack was busy, the other alphas were out on a new assignment, on protection duty for a visiting politician. I was glad that none of them were there.

As intimidating as Courtney can be on her own, the idea of Titan glaring at me, or Will sitting there with an eyebrow cocked, or Clay or Manny, interjecting while Courtney berated me would have pushed me over the line from nervous into nauseous.

I hated how nervous I was. It wasn't natural for a wolf, I knew, but I wasn't quite sure what to do about it either. Telling the truth usually helped. I hated lying.

But telling the truth in this case would get my best friend in trouble and he would likely kick my ass when it was all over.

"Chase," Courtney said again.

I sighed.

"He's with a girl, like I told you. He took her into the woods. She's his mate, he says." I frowned at myself for adding the "he says." It was just strange, when I met Cheyenne, I'd gotten a crazy strong feeling, a desire to kiss her. I'd met a lot of women I wanted to kiss in my life...but that feeling with Cheyenne was different.

It almost drove me to just do it without thinking. The more I thought about that, and from what I remembered growing up in the pack, that was one of the signs of meeting your mate. Between Ridge and me, I'm sure Cheyenne would pick Ridge anyways. I just needed to control my impulses once he brought her back to the compound, both out of respect and for my own safety. Ridge loved me, but what was his, was his. He didn't share, and if he cared about something or someone, he'd fight to the death for them.

"In the woods? Is she a wolf?"

My stomach felt like someone was stabbing a knife into it and I felt acid rising up in my throat as I said, "No. She's human."

"Son of a bitch!" Courtney said. "Did he drug her, Chase?" The "drug" was a light sedative, derived from a plant in the forest. Us shifters had used it to help with sleep or anxiety for years, eating the leaves right off the plant.

Somewhere along the way, one of us figured out how to extract the drug from the plant and encase it in an edible capsule and it had been used to "capture" human mates for years. Ridge had sent me to pick it up the last time I went into Bali for supplies. I had felt like a criminal, meeting with the seller in a dark alley.

The drug wasn't exactly illegal, but not exactly legal either. It wasn't on any kind of FDA or pharmaceutical data base, but they could figure out what it was and where it came from if they tried. I was sure I'd be charged with something if they caught me with it. But for Ridge, my best friend, and my hero most days, I'd do practically anything.

"I didn't see..."

"Cut the bullshit Chase. Did he drug her? I saw a poster at the post office in town today. There's a girl who's gone missing. Is it her? Is her name Cheyenne?"

I couldn't keep it in any longer.

Courtney would figure it out anyways and then I'd be in deeper shit. "Yes, he drugged her, and yes, it's Cheyenne." Just saying her name tickled my core. I had to get over that for sure or when Ridge did come back, he'd sense it.

He had better senses than any wolf I'd ever known, even the alphas. That's why when he said Cheyenne was his mate, I didn't doubt him, despite my own feelings otherwise.

"Shit!" Courtney jumped to her feet, grabbed the handle of the huge stroller her 3 babies were sleeping in and headed for the door of the meeting room. Their compound had one large cabin with a meeting room, a kitchen and a guest room.

The alphas and their three children had their own little cabin, Ridge, me and Grayson shared one, and there were a dozen or so more, shared in different ways among the rest of the pack. I continued to sit there after Courtney left, wondering how much trouble I was in. I figured it was pretty deep shit, and that's when I decided since I was already up a creek, I'd take it further and just throw the paddle over myself. I walked over to the back door of the cabin, cracked it open and sniffed the air. There was no scent of a wolf or a human and no sounds that anyone was around. I quickly stripped off my clothes and shifted. With the pups, Courtney would have to drive up to the cabin in the woods. I could get there faster the back way, on four legs. I was a fast wolf, one of the fastest on our compound. It was really the only thing I had to offer, but at least it was something. I knew Ridge was going to be pissed at me, but no more so than Courtney was and I'd survived that...so far.

"*L*et me go!" I had been alone with Ridge in a small cabin in the woods for at least two days. I was a little disoriented, since he refused to let me go outside. I'd tried to run, more than once.

I was halfway out one of the narrow windows one day when he caught me and another time, while he was sleeping, I'd stolen the key to the door.

At least I thought he was asleep. He let me get the key in the door before he grabbed me, put me back in my room and locked me in.

He was so maddeningly polite about it all too...at least most of the time.

I kicked him once, pretty hard in the shins and he growled at me. It was a literal growl, like an angry dog. That scared me, but not enough to lay down and be docile. If he was planning on raping or killing me, I would fight to the death. And if he was planning on any of that, I wished he'd just get it over with. Being locked up and not knowing what might happen was the worst kind of torture...at least that I knew so far.

"I'll let you go, if you promise to stop trying to run every time I open the door."

He had opened the door to bring in my food. I had to admit that he fed me well. The first day I refused to eat anything. I was afraid he was drugging me again. But my hunger got the best of me.

I was never one of those girls who picked at a salad and worried about calories...as evidenced by my "curvy" stature. He'd fed me barbecued rabbit for dinner last night and some kind of fish that was really tasty for breakfast this morning. But by lunch time I was antsy again, and when he opened the door I charged him.

Now the tray of food was scattered all over the floor and some of it was on the wall. He had caught me so easily too, it was almost embarrassing. One big arm around my waist had me lifted up off the floor and completely in his control.

"I won't promise anything!" I yelled defiantly. "How dare you do this to me? Who do you think you are? Put me down!"

He carried me over to the bed and dropped me.

The bed indented and I bounced up and back down. As soon as I stopped moving, I tried to get back up again. Ridge sat down and took hold of my wrists, pressing me down into the bed and putting his face right in front of mine.

"Stop this."

"Why don't you just get it over with?"

"Get what over with, my love?"

"Don't call me that! I am not your love! I think you're a little bit crazy. Just do whatever you brought me here to do and get it over with. Rape me or kill me or boil me in your stew...whatever! Just do it!"

He was laughing. It really pissed me off when he did that, like my anger entertained him. "Boil you in my stew? Do I look like a cannibal? I'm hurt."

"Oh, I'm so sorry. I didn't know kidnapping maniacs got their feelings hurt."

"You're so feisty." He was grinning, like we were on a date and he was giving me a compliment.

"And I won't stop fighting, ever. So just shoot me already, or slit my throat or..."

"Cheyenne, stop. I'm not going to kill you."

"Then what do you want from me?"

"I want you to be mine...my mate."

It was my turn to throw my head back and laugh. When I finished laughing I said, "How pathetic are you that you have to kidnap a woman to convince her to be your...mate? And why do you call it that? It makes you sound like a...like a..."

"An animal?" he said with a sarcastic grin. I narrowed my eyes and said, "Excuse me?"

"An animal. Mate, sounds like talking about an animal's better half. Which is what I'm..." The sound of the door opening in the outer room got both of our attention. He jumped to his feet and I started screaming.

"Help! Help me! He's holding me hostage!" Ridge reached down and placed one of his giant hands over my mouth. I tried to bite him, but he was pressing down too hard. I brought my hands up to scratch at him and I heard a voice from the other room say,

"Ridge! Is everything okay in there?"

Relief washed over me.

Surely there couldn't be two of them crazy enough to believe they could get away with this. I wasn't encouraged by the fact that Ridge took his hand off my mouth. That told me that he wasn't afraid of whoever was in the other room, finding out that I was in here. "Everything's fine, Chase. Don't open the door. I'll be right out."

"Chase? Your cute little friend is in on this too?"

Ridge's features changed suddenly.

The look on his face grew much darker and the frown he held caused a deep line to appear out of nowhere between his eyebrows. "You think Chase is cute?"

"Are you kidding? Are we in middle school again?" He turned his head sideways as he looked into my eyes, like he was trying to understand what I said. I thought it was simple and self-explanatory. He had me hostage and he was going to worry about me calling his friend "cute".

"Do you?" he asked again.

"You're insane."

There was a knock on the door and Chase's voice sounded urgent as he said, "Ridge, I need to talk to you, now!"

Ridge rolled his eyes and looked back down at me. "Don't move," he said. I sneered at him as he got up. He walked backward to the door, making sure I wasn't going to charge him. I waited until he opened the door and I got a glimpse of Chase on the other side, he was naked.

What the hell?

I felt my head spin. Was he here to join in on the rape and torture? Why else would he be naked? My thoughts were racing and tears were streaming down my face.

Every so often I had to let out a sob and I hated that. I didn't want to appear weak to him, or his naked friend. They were out there plotting and soon, they'd be back in here...with me. I wasn't going to let them rape me. I had to find a way out and I had to do it now...

"Courtney is really pissed."

"I can't believe you gave me up that easily. I never had you figured for a snitch, Chase." I felt bad calling him a snitch. I knew as soon as I took Cheyenne that when they pressured him, he would crack.

It was his nature to be honest and to be honest myself, I was impressed that it took him two days. I wasn't going to tell him that though.

"Damn it, Ridge! She had it all figured out already. There are posters of Cheyenne's face in the post office in town. She disappeared at the same time you did. You're not answering your phone. Did you think you'd just waltz back in with a mate in a week and no one would notice?"

"Once she's mine there won't be anything anyone can do about it. Once she changes...there's no going back."

"Do you know for sure that you can even change her?" Chase hit an exposed nerve with that one. We had both lost our pack so young, before we had reached the age of maturity, where the elders took us aside and explained it all to us.

I'd seen the mating rituals growing up. I'd watched them

bite each other underneath the full moon and become as one...but I'd never seen it happen with a human. I'd heard tales of how female humans were taken and bitten and changed, but I honestly had no idea if a bite was all there was to it.

That's why I hadn't bitten Cheyenne yet. I wanted to make sure I got it right on the first try.

"I can change her," I said, more confidently than I felt. "I'm waiting for the moon to be full tomorrow night."

"Then why didn't you wait and take her tomorrow night?" Chase asked.

"Because she goes to the club on Friday nights. It was the safest place to take her. I'm sure her employer has cameras set up and she lives with a roommate in an apartment complex."

Chase was pacing and every time he heard a sob come from the other room, he stopped and looked in that direction with a distressed look on his face. "Is she okay?" he asked. "Is she eating?"

"What kind of monster do you think I am? I've caught a rabbit or fish or squirrel every day and I even cooked it for her. She's eating well, and she's fine. She just doesn't understand yet that this is what she wants, but she will."

Chase snorted and shook his head. "Sometimes your confidence borders on arrogance. What if she doesn't want this? You're not just talking about changing her. You're talking about changing her and everything she knows to be true, Ridge. What if it makes her miserable? Will you be okay with that?"

"I can sense that she wants me, as much as I want her. She'll come around to it soon, I guarantee you she will."

"None of that matters. Courtney will be here in a few minutes, and unless you want to go back to being a lone wolf, you better be ready to do whatever she says to clean up this mess."

"I'm not giving up my mate," I said, stubbornly.

Chase started to say something else, but the sound of the pack's Jeep driving up out front, had both of our attention. Chase's eyes were wide. He looked like he was the one about to get kicked out of the pack. If that was the worst that Courtney had planned for me, I could live with it, as long as I had Cheyenne.

I braced myself as Courtney stormed inside.

She was carrying the baby carrier and I could hear one of the babies cooing inside.

I almost chuckled at the thought of our fearless alpha, taking her pup or sometimes all of her pups to work with her. Luckily for me, I was smart enough not to underestimate our alpha.

She was strong and smart and capable enough to lead an entire pack made up mostly of men. She never backed down from a fight, or a challenge and judging from the fire in her eyes now, I knew I had to be ready for both.

"What in the hell are you doing? Have you lost your damned mind?" She spun on Chase before I had a chance to answer and said, "And you! You tell me where he is and then race up here to warn him? Were you plotting to get him out of here with the girl and I got here too fast?"

"No Courtney, I..." She was finished with him, for the time being.

She turned back on me and said, "Well? You've got two seconds to explain yourself. This will be your one and only chance before I meet with my mates and we decide what your punishment will be for this. You've put the fate of our entire pack in jeopardy, Ridge...do you even realize that?"

"She's my mate, Courtney. Once I change her..."

"Change her? You brought her here to change her, against her will?"

"No! I thought after a few days she would warm up to me. I know she has to go into this willingly. I just needed some time to...convince her."

Courtney sat the baby carrier down. "I had such high hopes for you, Ridge. Let me talk to her."

"Courtney...please understand. She's my mate. I know she is just as clearly as you knew who yours were."

"None of my mates tried to force anything on me, Ridge. That's the difference. This is our home, or it was. What do you think will happen when this girl goes back and tells everyone you kidnapped her? Our business here will be ruined. Our lives here will be ruined. You made a one-sided decision that affects this entire pack and unless I can think of a way to smooth this over...our downfall is on you. Now, unlock that door and let me talk to her. Chase, take the baby out to the car. There's a pair of emergency sweat pants and a sweatshirt in the back. Get dressed and wait for me there. The keys are in it if he wakes up, he likes to listen to the radio. We don't need the shock of seeing your white ass making things worse."

Chase put his head down in shame as he picked up the baby carrier and headed outside.

I was trying to think of some way to refuse what Courtney was telling me, but it was hopeless. I'd never fight her, and even if I did, she had four alpha mates who would have me in pieces just minutes afterwards. I took the key to the door out of my jeans and walked over and unlocked it.

I expected Cheyenne to charge me again and when she didn't, I stuck my head in the room.

The door to the little bathroom was open. I walked over to it with Courtney on my heels and stopped dead in my tracks when I got there.

"I'll be a son of a bitch." The toilet was the kind specifically manufactured for a motor home or trailer. It was light and when the cabin was constructed, it had simply been positioned on top of the hole that emptied down into the sewer underneath.

The toilet was sitting in the bathtub and Cheyenne, was gone.

I couldn't let myself think about what I'd just waded through or I'd be too sick to run. I had nearly lost my lunch when I lowered myself down into that hole. The worst part was that I had to duck my head under and push up through the pump that was set up alongside the house.

I couldn't think about that though, I had to get far enough away that they couldn't find me, and go from there. I didn't know which way to go.

The trees and foliage around me all looked the same. I looked up at the sun which was getting low in the sky, like the afternoon was going to turn to evening soon.

It was bright and looked like it was about to descend down behind the mountains. I pictured the little town on the island.

The mountains were to the west, and the beach to the east. I had to go away from the sun which would take me right past the front of the house. I didn't have any other choice though. If I got up deeper in the mountains before the sun went down, I'd be lost for sure, out in the night with God knows what kind of creepy, crawly things, or wild beasts.

Dripping with funk of the sort I'd never imagined I would be bathed in, I began to jog along the side of the cabin, stopping at the edge of it and sticking my head around to make sure the coast was clear. I was shocked when I saw the Jeep, and even more surprised that it was running. I was about 12 or 14 feet away from it and I could see the front driver and passenger seats.

There was no one in there...they'd left me an escape vehicle.

Maybe.

What if it was a trap?

I was torn.

I knew I should just keep running, but I had no idea where I was or how far I was from town. There were too many variables in the little island jungle at night.

When I first moved there, I was warned about a population of wolves that lived near the mountains, and different species of poisonous spiders and snakes. Things that could kill me before I even knew they were there. I decided to chance that someone had just stopped by, and maybe didn't know Ridge was harboring a captive.

It was my best shot.

I wasn't a runner, never have been. But I ran toward that Jeep faster than I'd ever run in my life. I was practically still in motion as I grabbed the door handle and pulled it open, swinging myself up into the vehicle practically in one motion.

It's amazing what you are capable of when adrenaline was pumping through your veins.

I threw the Jeep into drive without even closing the side door and floored the accelerator. The radio was on and between the loud music and the roar of the engine, not to mention the roar of the blood in my head, I didn't hear a thing. I flew down the dirt path until I came to a windy, paved road. I was moving the Jeep around those curves as fast as it would go when I reached up and adjusted the rear-view mirror...and saw a pair of green eyes, filled with fear, staring at me from the back seat.

I screamed, he let out a bizarre little sound and then as I slammed on the breaks in the first clearing I came to, a baby started to cry.

CHASE

I was surprised when Cheyenne jumped in the car, but even more surprised at how badly she smelled. I was going to say something when she first floored it and took off, but she was flying down the hill so fast, I was afraid to startle her. I looked over at the precious cargo next to me.

So far, the 10-month-old baby was sleeping...like a baby. It was only when Cheyenne slammed on the brakes and started to scream that the baby woke up and chimed in himself.

"What the hell is that?" Cheyenne screamed.

I reached over and unbuckled the baby and took him out of the seat. "Just a baby," I told her, holding the little man up and turning him so he was facing her. "See."

"Jesus!" she said, with her hand over her heart. "Whose baby is that?"

"He belongs to our...to the employers of the company Ridge and I work for. His name is..."

"I don't care what his name is. Take him and get out."

"Seriously? You're going to put me and this innocent little baby out along the side of the road?"

"I was kidnapped. I swam through shit to escape. You were in on it. Get! Out!"

I sighed and put the baby back in his carrier. He started to cry again while I buckled him into his seat. I was taking my time and Cheyenne realized it. "Hurry!" she snapped.

"I think he's hungry. I need his diaper bag up there on the passenger seat..."

"There's no bag here. Get out! You can call for a ride once you're out. He'll be fine."

"Oh, there's no cell phone service up here..."

"Then walk back to the cabin. Your buddy is there, and whoever belongs to that baby too, I guess. Is your entire company twisted and in on this? What's your end game? I don't know anyone with money to pay a ransom."

"It's not about ransom. Ridge likes you."

Cheyenne laughed, a sad, squeaky sound. "Well, I guess that answers my question about why he's single."

"We do things a little...differently," I told her, "But honestly, Ridge doesn't mean you any harm."

"He has a funny way of showing that...all of it. But, I don't want to hear excuses. Get out, now, and take that baby with you."

"Can I get the bag out of the back?"

"Get out!" Before she finished yelling those two words, the baby was crying again and the passenger door was pulled open.

She was obviously surprised to see Courtney standing there. Courtney wrinkled her nose, probably at the smell in the Jeep. I was sure I'd get the job of cleaning it out when we got back to the compound, and that would only be one of my punishments. "Leave me alone," Cheyenne yelled at her.

"I'm not going to hurt you," Courtney said, "I'm here to help you."

It was obvious that Cheyenne didn't trust her. At this

point, I would be surprised if she trusted anyone. "If that's your baby, you better take him now, or I'm taking him with me. Either way, I'm getting out of here."

"Cheyenne, I can't let you do that until we have a chance to talk, okay?"

"No! Not okay..." the door opened behind her and before she could react, Ridge grabbed her around the waist and pulled her out.

She was kicking and screaming and Ridge was trying to wrestle her around so that he could get his hand over her mouth. When I took the baby and got out of the Jeep, it was just in time to hear Ridge yelp in pain and see Cheyenne with a mouthful of his flesh. He tried to pull his hand away, but it looked like she was biting down harder. I saw the transformation.

It was likely caused by pain and rage, but Ridge lost control for just a second. His hazel eyes flashed yellow and his canines dropped.

Cheyenne had to have noticed because she let go of him and suddenly she was as still as a statue. She stared at him for several seconds, then opened her mouth full of blood and began to scream again.

It was only when Courtney screamed "Stop! Enough!" in what the rest of us in the pack refer to as her demon voice, that she suddenly stopped.

The baby stopped crying too and Ridge and I both froze. That was Courtney's "I mean business" voice and if anyone didn't comply, there would be consequences.

Once everyone was quiet and calm, Courtney began snapping orders. "Chase, take the baby back up to the house in the Jeep. The other two are there with the midwife, you can leave him there. Cheyenne, are you going to walk nicely or do I have to have Ridge carry you?"

"I'll walk," she said, pulling out of Ridge's grasp. I felt a tickle of sympathy for my friend. I'd never seen him look so sad. He knew that no matter how this turned out that he'd probably ruined any chance he may have ever had with the woman he was sure was his mate.

The woman gave Ridge a hard stare and with a huff, he began to follow me. She fell into step with me and said, "My name is Courtney. I'm one of the owners of The Pack Security Services."

"Well, this is a fine way to run a business," I said, sarcastically.

She looked at Ridge again like she wanted to bite his head off, but in a calm voice she said, "This isn't about our business. Ridge is a...friend, and I came here to help him."

"Help him? It would seem that I'm the one who needs help. I've been held captive for at least two days and I'm covered in human feces."

Courtney wrinkled her perfect little nose and said, "Yeah, sorry about that. I'm here to help you too. But first, let's let you get cleaned up, then, we'll all sit down and talk."

"And what if I don't want to talk? I want to go home. I don't want to "talk" to my captor and his "friends.""

"We'll get you home safely, I promise. Just give me this much and I'll get you wherever you need to go, unharmed."

I wanted to scream again, but I controlled it. I walked

faster and by the time we made it back to the little house, the...stuff I was covered with began to get hard and crusty. I was feeling sicker to my stomach by the minute.

Courtney opened the door and Chase was sitting there in a rocking chair, holding the boy baby. The little guy had fallen asleep on his shoulder.

I hated to admit it, but they were kind of cute. "Go ahead and shower, Cheyenne. There should be everything you need in there. I have some clothes in the jeep. I'll get them for you." I looked at Courtney's small frame and raised an eyebrow. She smiled and said, "I'm sure I have something to fit you. Please though, don't take off again. I promise you'll be home very soon."

I didn't respond to that.

If it wasn't a matter of swimming through shit again only to get caught a second time, I might try it again. I went into the bathroom and had to pull the toilet out of the tub before starting the shower. Once the water warmed up, I got in with my clothes on first. I scrubbed my pants and blouse with soap and once they were halfway clean, I peeled them off and showered myself. It felt so good to wash the literal shit out of my hair and off my face.

I stayed in the shower until every last drop of hot water was used up, and then I finally stepped out and began to dry off.

There was a knock on the door when I was just about finished drying. "It's Courtney. I left the clothes on the bed." I didn't respond. What was I going to do, thank her? I wasn't thanking any of them, for any of this. I was getting angrier by the minute just thinking about it.

Chase and Courtney had not come here to save me. If that were the case, they would have brought the police. They came here to save him...and that really pissed me off.

I finished drying off and went into the bedroom and

found the clothes she'd left for me. There was red and blue flannel shirt and a pair of gray sweat pants. Not exactly stylish, but warm, dry, and not covered in feces. I put them on and then reluctantly, opened the bedroom door.

Courtney had one of the babies in her lap now. Chase was starting a fire in the fire place, still with one on his hip. The other was asleep in the crib in the corner, and Ridge was sitting on the couch with a sullen look on his face. I avoided eye-contact with him and looked at Courtney. "Okay. Can we get this over with so I can get home, please?"

"Sure," she said, handing the baby she held over to Chase who put him on his other hip, like it was natural. "Will you have a seat?" I looked at Ridge, narrowing my eyes at him, and then walked past him to sit down in the other chair. I wasn't about to sit next to him on the couch. I sat down and folded my arms across my chest.

Courtney looked at Ridge and then back to me and said, "You may not believe this, but Ridge is really a nice guy." I snorted and Courtney actually smiled. "I get that you're not going to believe that, but I promise you there's a lot more to him than what you've seen the past two days. What Ridge really is, is confused. He likes you, and he went about trying to get you to like him back, entirely the wrong way."

"You think?"

She chuckled at that. "I'm sorry. I wish this was easier to explain. Ridge was raised in a world where things were done very differently than what we consider "normal".

"Where?" I asked, "In the wild?"

Suddenly the smile was no longer on Courtney's face. I wasn't looking at Ridge but I could see him out of the corner of my eye and I saw him shift in his seat.

A few seconds passed and she finally said, "Well to be honest, yes." I looked at him then. He was looking at me with those intense hazel eyes of his, but he didn't speak.

It was Courtney who went on and I realized suddenly that she was as crazy as he was, and I was stupid for not taking off again when I had the chance. "Ridge is a wolf-shifter, we all are."

"Excuse me?"

"Most lay people think of us as werewolves. It's not quite the same thing..."

"Stop," I said, putting my palms up. "Please stop. This is your excuse for this man kidnapping me? You're werewolves?"

"Shifters," Chase said.

"Hush Chase," Courtney snapped at him.

"This is crazy."

"I agree that it sounds crazy. I didn't believe it myself at first..."

"So, you're not a werewolf?" I couldn't even believe I was having this conversation. My head felt like it was going to explode.

"Yes, I'm a wolf-shifter too, but I wasn't always. I met my mates after they had been changed and..."

"Wait, whoa, this just gets crazier. Did you say "mates"?

"Yes. I have four mates."

I couldn't help it at that point. I started laughing like a crazy person. When I finally stopped I looked at Ridge and said, "Man, can I pick them."

"Cheyenne..." he started.

"No. I told Courtney I'd hear her out. I don't want to hear anything else from you. Courtney, I heard you out. Can I go now?"

"Well, there's the matter of what you're going to tell people. A lot of people are looking for you and probably very worried. They're going to want to know what happened to you. The police were called in from Bali today because it's been 48 hours..."

"What do you want me to tell them?" I asked. These people were genuinely crazy. At that point I would have promised them anything just to get the hell out of there.

"Maybe that you were drunk and you wandered too far from the club, and got lost?" I could tell by the look on her face that she realized how lame that story sounded. But it didn't matter, as soon as I was out of here, I was telling the police everything, before these crazy people hurt somebody.

"Sure, okay. Can I go now?"

"One more thing," Courtney said. "We're not bad people. We're not violent people. We just want to live our lives, raise our families and get along the way everyone else does. Ridge is learning new ways to live. Being human was a much smaller part of his life than being wolf was. In the wild if a wolf finds his mate, he just takes her. Ridge knows what he did was wrong though, and he won't bother you again, isn't that right, Ridge?"

We both looked at him. His eyes were on me. I hated that I still felt a tingle in my belly when he looked at me. I stifled a shudder and finally Courtney repeated his name and he said, "Yes. Right." He didn't sound convincing, but again, he wouldn't be running around free after I spoke to the police.

"Fine. Can I go now?"

"Chase?" I didn't even realize Chase left the room. I looked around when she called him and for a few seconds, I thought I was losing my own mind. A big, beautiful gray wolf sauntered into the room from the kitchen. I was sure my face must have been as white as a ghost and my jaw was dragging the floor. Courtney was looking at me and she said, "He won't hurt you, but I wanted to be sure before you went home and told your story, that you knew what you were dealing with."

Suddenly I felt rage again. She was threatening me. "How dare you? You send Chase out of the room and he sends in your pet wolf so not only do you believe I'll buy into your threats but I'm an idiot as well..."

Courtney was standing up as I was going off.

I saw her look at the wolf and then suddenly the strangest thing began to happen to her face. The bones seemed to be stretching and her muscles were rippling.

I watched it like a train wreck, unable to turn away as white hair began to sprout all over her body. The whole process only took seconds, but I felt like I'd witnessed it in slow motion. Suddenly a white wolf, smaller than the gray one was standing where Courtney had been. I turned my head toward the gray wolf and that was when the scream escaped my throat.

I thought Cheyenne was going to faint dead away. I wouldn't have blamed her, having to look at Chase naked. He was whiter than Courtney's fur.

If I didn't know better, I would think he hadn't seen the sun in years. Go figure, my mate would get to see him naked first.

At least he's no competition.

He cupped his hands in front of his penis and said, "I'm sorry, Cheyenne, I'll put some clothes on." Cheyenne's breaths were fast and deep and her eyes were as wide as saucers. I'm not sure she even heard Chase since she was staring at Courtney.

Courtney gave her a minute or two to look her over and then she shifted back into herself. I automatically took the afghan off the couch and handed it to her. Courtney is beautiful, but she doesn't belong to me and I shouldn't be looking at her like that. She wrapped the blanket around her shoulders and told Cheyenne,

"I'm sorry to frighten you, but there's no other way to prove that we're not crazy...we're wolves. Are you okay?"

Cheyenne looked like she didn't know if she should scream again, run, or cry. Instead, she nodded dumbly and after a few more seconds she said, "I won't tell anyone, I promise. Please, just let me go home."

Courtney nodded. "I'm sorry for all we've put you through. We'll take you home right now."

I was surprised that Courtney was going to let me anywhere near Cheyenne, so I wasn't surprised when I stood up and she said, "You can run home with Chase. I'll take her."

I wanted to argue.

I desperately wanted a chance to be close to Cheyenne again so that I could see if that spark was still as strong as it was.

But I knew I'd only be getting myself into deeper trouble. I just nodded at Courtney and tried to look at Cheyenne, but she wouldn't look at me still. I left her there with Courtney and went into the kitchen where Chase had gone. I wasn't sure what would happen from here on out, but I was sure that if they forced me to stay away from her, they might have to put me in a cage to make sure I complied.

* * *

"I've never been into humans," the old wolf said as he stuffed another handful of chips in his mouth.

They'd picked up the old wolf around the same time they found Chase.

He never told me exactly how old he was, but if I had to guess I'd put him around eighty. We were on a stake out, on a Friday night.

For the past three weeks, I hated Friday nights. I longed to see Cheyenne again and thinking about those nights at the club, just sitting and talking to her and gazing into her beautiful eyes was killing me. Before I even realized what I was doing, I started to talk about her...and I even told my partner for the night, an old guy named Granite, that I'd lost my mind, drugged and kidnapped her. The rest of the pack didn't know about all that. The alphas had kept it all between us and I was grateful. As the days passed, I felt guiltier about what I had done.

It was the way of my ancestors, but times had changed and I knew I had to grow and change along with them.

"So all these extra shifts you've been doing, and those toilets I saw you fixing on the compound...all that was your punishment for what you did?"

"Yeah. Extra shifts, less pay, dirty jobs and the threat of being expelled if anything like this ever happens again." It was infuriating to be told what to do like a child, but these were orders that I was afraid I couldn't afford to defy.

Being a lone wolf is about as risky as things can get for one of us. We need our pack to sustain our lives and continue to hide our identities from the humans that would come at us with the figurative pitch forks and torches.

But sadly, if I thought there was any chance I'd still end up with Cheyenne I might take the risk. I hated to give up, but she had been so incredibly freaked out that day three weeks ago when Courtney took her home that I was sure she'd run screaming in the other direction if we ever came face to face. I suppose the good news was that she had made up a story about where she was those two days and as far as we could tell, she hadn't told a soul about us.

"I never really knew a human, before Courtney, Clay, Will, Titan and Manny," I told him, trying to think of something that would keep me from talking about her...and how badly I wanted her, still.

"I've known plenty of them," Granite said. "There was this one hooker down in Memphis...human as they come, but this chick was into wolves. She used to give us a fifty percent discount if we'd agree to change for her before we left at the end of the night. I guess everybody has their preferences, and their fetishes."

I chuckled and said, "So Granite, why don't you have a mate?"

"I had mine, son. My Racine and I were together for fifty years before our pack was discovered and we were forced out of Memphis. We lived for a while in the Black Hills, but the winters were hell and the pack was slowly dying off. Moved from there to Arkansas back in '95, but got caught up in a war between two packs and lost a bunch more of our younger people. Racine got sick there, got a bad case of Lyme disease. Normally, our immune systems can fight off just about anything, but my sweet Racine was already up there in years and all the travels had caused her to lose a lot of weight...her poor body just couldn't handle all of it. I lost her on the way to California. By the time we got to Mexico it was only me and one of the pups left in the pack. We stowed away on a boat and ended up in Australia for a while."

I didn't question what he was doing with the hooker in Memphis if he had, his "Racine," not out loud anyways.

"You have a pup?"

He looked sad as he said,"I did. You know Australia doesn't have any wolves, indigenous ones, anyways. So the dingoes weren't too happy to see us. The problem with the dingoes are how sneaky they are. The sons of bitches attacked us in our sleep, 8 of them. The boy was amazing. He fought off at least five of them on his own. When all was said and done, there were six dead dingoes and the other two ran off and didn't come back. We were both pretty torn up, but I've always healed quickly and I guess I just assumed the boy would too. He seemed to be healing, but one of his wounds got infected and within days, he was gone. After that I was just lost, wandering the world with no purpose...and then the Pack found me. I tell you boy, you don't ever want to go off alone. It's a harsh world we live in."

I nodded.

I knew he was right, but at the same time I spent so much of my time feeling all alone. All I ever wanted was a family, besides my pack, a mate and some pups of my own. My thoughts were interrupted by the motion of the door we'd been watching all day. It was finally swinging open. We were hired by an insurance company that thought there was something fishy about a payout they'd recently made to a widow on the island.

The police had done an investigation when the man's car went off the side of a cliff and ended in a fiery crash. His body was burned beyond recognition and he was declared dead. The insurance wrote a hefty check to the widow, and then almost immediately hired us.

According to Clay, they think the man faked his own death. We had been watching his widow for two weeks. She sure didn't seem to be grieving at all.

She was busy all the time...spending all that money on having her home redecorated, buying a new car and taking a lot of trips to the mainland to shop for designer clothes and jewelry.

But, we hadn't seen any sign of her husband, or any man in her life...at first. Then one day when I was watching the house, the man who tended to the lawn and garden arrived.

The problem was that he wasn't the same man we had photos of, the same man who had been doing it all along.

He was heavier, and older when I pulled up the photo of McAvoy on my phone and started to compare the two. The caretaker had a thinner nose than McAvoy, different color hair and eyes and a scar on his cheek, but I would still swear it was the same man. I ran that by the alphas and after careful scrutiny of the photos, they all agreed. It was a good day, I think I gained back some respect that I'd lost.

They didn't want to grab him up right away however. They wanted to watch him, and the wife for a while longer and see what kind of case we could build against them, hopefully a tight one, that their money wouldn't help them out of. So tonight, Courtney and Grayson were watching her, and Granite and I, him.

We had found out he was staying in a warehouse down near the docks that was owned by his ex-partner, but so far, he went straight to the warehouse after his days at the mansion and never left until the next day when he headed back over and pretended to be a landscaper. At least not until tonight.

"Give me the binoculars, someone's moving over there." Granite handed the binoculars to me and I trained them on the figure coming out of the warehouse door. It was McAvoy, in a trench coat. I watched him put a padlock on the warehouse door, and I wondered not for the first time, what he was hiding in there.

Before he left, he took a look around him like he was making sure he was alone and then head toward a golf cart that sat near the front of the small parking lot. "He's getting in the golf cart. You think we should approach on foot or follow him?"

"I say follow him for a bit," Granite said. "Let's see what he's up to."

I picked up my phone and texted Clay that he was on the move and we were following, handed the binoculars back to Granite and waited for the golf cart to pull out on the narrow frontage road before starting the car. I let him get a good lead and then I began to follow after him.

He drove along the frontage road for a while until he came to a small gravel path that there was no way I'd be able to take the Jeep down. I parked it and as I was getting out, I heard Granite open his door. "Why don't you stay here?"

"I'm old, boy, not dead." I wasn't going to argue with him. I tucked my gun into my jeans and started up the path when suddenly, I smelled a wolf. I looked behind me and there was Granite, an old brown wolf, trotting up behind me. I shook my head and kept going. There were situations that called for shifting but I thought this one called more for carrying a gun. I guess a sharp mouthful of teeth, and twenty or so razor claws couldn't hurt as back-up no matter what we encountered out here in the dark.

The taillights on the golf cart had disappeared into the dark countryside but I could see what looked like a storage or guard shack up ahead. I listened closely to the night and stepped lightly on the gravel so as not to make too much noise as we approached. I could see Granite sniffing the air and I knew that although my senses were enhanced even in human form, they were nowhere near as strong as they were when I shifted. I was glad that Granite had, especially as we got closer and I was sure that I could smell more than one human. I looked down at Granite and held up two fingers.

The old wolf picked up his front paw and scratched at the ground. "One, two, three, four." Shit. I slid my phone out of my pocket and trying to hide the light from it underneath my jacket, I sent Clay a text.

"Followed subject from warehouse approximately four miles to another dwelling. Smell multiple humans. Should we go in, or abort?"

I got down on one knee next to Granite to make my shadow less noticeable in case anyone stepped out, and I waited. A few seconds went by and I got a message from Clay that said,

"On our way. Don't go in until we get there. If subject or anyone else comes out, follow but don't approach."

The hair on the back of my neck was standing up. Something about this was off, but I couldn't put my finger on what it was.

We were careful, but there was always the possibility that he'd made us, following him. If they came out now, Granite and I were not only outnumbered, but there was no place to really hide. I looked at the back of the little house and motioned to the wolf. He followed me up to the cabin, him stepping lightly and me practically crawling.

Once there, we crouched close to the edge where we could still see any movement from either side, and waited. It seemed like an eternity before I smelled Clay and Manny coming up the path behind me.

If not for their smell however, I wouldn't have ever known they were there. When they reached me and Granite, Clay said, "Any movement?"

I shook my head. "Nothing."

"Do we know if there's an exit on the other side?" Manny asked, sniffing the air.

"No. We stayed put like we were told," I told him. "I can still smell them though."

"Something's off," Manny said, "About the smell."

I sniffed the air again, and so did Clay. I could still smell humans. Clay frowned, and for a second I questioned my own senses, but then he said, "I smell them. What's off about it?"

I was relieved that he smelled them too, and I wasn't dead wrong. I wanted to gain their respect back, and I was on my way to doing that. I still wasn't sure what to do about my feelings for Cheyenne, but at least I could throw myself into work, and do a great job.

"I smell death," Manny said. "Human death."

I closed my eyes and smelled the air. I can always pick up decomposition, it's the worst smell in the world. I was disappointed in myself because I still simply smelled humans. I guess they could be dead, but the bodies had to be fresh.

The other strange thing was that there was no smell of blood in the air. In the case of dead humans, shot or stabbed or even in a car accident… the scent was usually strong.

Suddenly the smell was forgotten when I heard movement from the direction of the front of the shed. Everyone did, apparently.

Clay and I were on one side, still crouched low, but now with guns ready. Manny was on the other side with Granite at his knee, the brown hair on his back standing straight up all over.

Clay made eye-contact with me and then looked over at Manny and Granite before standing up slowly and waving his arm for them to advance. Manny slipped around one side with Granite on his heels and Clay slipped around the other and I followed him.

I'd been involved in many of the security jobs we'd taken on, but none with the possibility of a gunfight. My adrenaline was surging and my heart was pounding. I had my gun out and I was clutching it so tightly that I could feel my hand tingling as the blood tried to make its way through.

We made it around the side, almost to the center of the wall of the shed when a shadow suddenly appeared from around the front of the house. Before we could even process that, a volley of shots broke the silence of the night.

Clay and I hit the ground, and returned fire. The man dove back behind the house, but we heard gunfire from that direction...and then suddenly, nothing.

Manny got him, or he got Manny...but that was doubtful. We heard a low whistle and if there was any doubt, that settled it. We made our way the rest of the way around and there was McAvoy...truly dead now, with a hole in the center of his chest. Manny was already on the porch and ready to open the door of the cabin.

Granite was standing by, but since he was still in wolf form, I went to help. Manny and I had our weapons ready as he kicked in the door. Clay was covering us from behind as we stepped into the doorway, guns drawn.

My heart was racing, but there was no need to worry. Every one inside was already dead.

Four men lay on the floor in the center of the room, one piled on top of the other in a stack. They were all nude, and now that I was close I could smell, obviously dead. I didn't smell blood and I didn't see any; their bodies seemed to be intact, at least what I could see. Maybe they'd been strangled, or poisoned, but whatever happened was recent and that's why Clay and I hadn't yet been able to pick up the smell of death.

We searched the rest of the place. It was only one room with a bathroom, so it didn't take any time at all to realize it was clear, save for the bodies. Counting the one outside, we now had five bodies, and I knew that it was going to be a long ass night.

CHEYENNE

"You know we love you, Chey, but it's been three weeks and you're as nervous as a cat all the time and only leave the house to go to work. I think something happened to you that night that you're not telling us."

Marta and Bonnie had ambushed me on Saturday morning, before I'd even had my coffee. I'd been so jumpy for the past three weeks, scared of my own shadow, that when I stepped out of my room and found them waiting for me in the living room, I actually screamed.

I walked past the both to the little kitchen as I said, "You just startled me is all. You shouldn't sneak up on a person first thing in the morning."

I got a mug out and began to pour my coffee.

The kitchen and living room are separated only by an island. I was wishing it were a wall when I realized they were both turned backwards on the couch, staring at me.

"This is us, Cheyenne. We only want to help you," Bonnie said.

"I don't need any help. I got drunk, wandered around lost

for a while, woke up in the woods and came home embarrassed as hell. I'll get over it."

"That story doesn't even make sense. What did you eat, drink? Where did you sleep for two nights? Those woods are full of creepy-crawling creatures. You expect us to believe you just curled up and slept on the ground?"

"Yes, I do. If you love me as much as you say you do, you'll believe me. I already have to deal with the daily calls from my mother, urging me to come home. I feel lucky I was even able to convince her and my father to not come out here. Do me a favor and next time I go missing, please don't call them."

Bonnie rolled her eyes as I walked back through the living room, trying to make it back to my room.

I was surprised when Marta stepped in front of my door.

"Uh uh," she said, "You've been avoiding this conversation for weeks and things are only getting worse. Bonnie says you're even distracted at work all the time, looking out the window and jumping every time the bells on the door ring. You have to tell us what really happened."

I sighed. I wanted to growl, or scream even. I just wanted them to leave me alone.

I had nightmares about hairy beasts every night. I was scared to death that they were coming to get me...and at the same time, I couldn't get Ridge off my mind. Not the Ridge that kidnapped me, but the man from the bar.

The hot, funny, sweet, interesting man that I truly thought liked me. I knew it was crazy to think anything about him, or feel anything toward him other than anger...but those crazy feelings like I belonged with him still ate away at me.

Go figure, I'd fall for a man who was part animal, and who would rather hold me captive in the woods than take me out on a real date. I feel like I'm losing my mind some days, and I want to talk about it.

But then I picture them...all three of them, turning into wolves in front of my eyes, and Courtney's veiled threats. What confused me most was when I pictured Chase, or Courtney with those babies... They were so soft and loving towards them... How could they be both monster and nurturer? None of it made any sense and I longed for the old days when I was simply a chubby, plain girl with a boring life.

"I already did," I said. "Now if you don't mind, it's my day off and I'd like to spend some time organizing my closet today."

"No." Marta said, folding her arms across her chest.

I raised my eyebrows at her. "No?"

"No." she said. Bonnie came over and stood next to her. Great, my roommate and my co-worker were going to push me around now too. "You're going to tell us the truth, Chey."

"Please," Bonnie said, "We love you. We can't let you go on like this." It was like an intervention. They were telling me, in a way, that I'd have no peace unless I told them "the truth".

My mind was racing as I tried to think of a story to tell them that would satisfy their curiosity, but I was coming up blank until Marta said,

"That guy, Ridge...he hasn't been back to the club since that night. I told the police about him when they finally came out, but because he works for the Pack, I don't think they even looked into it. Did he do something to you, Cheyenne? Please tell us, it's okay."

"No. I mean," I turned my back to them and walked toward the couch. I was a terrible liar. I'd told the one about wandering in the woods, drunk, until I almost believed it...but now I had to start all over.

It made my stomach hurt. I took a deep breath and said, "He didn't do anything to me, as in, hurt me. But..." I sat down and they practically rushed over and sat in the recliners opposite me.

Their eyes were wide, like they were about to hear some racy gossip...so, I decided to give them some. "I left with him that night, and I wasn't drunk."

Marta and Bonnie exchanged a look and Bonnie said, "Okay...and?"

"I live with a roommate, he lives with a roommate...so, we went looking for a place where we could...be alone."

Marta's mouth was hanging open. "You had sex? For two days?"

I nodded and I probably looked ashamed.

It wasn't about the "sex" however, it was the shame of telling such an outrageous lie. "We went to a place his friend owns in the woods...and we had, amazing, incredible, hot sex. I lost track of time. For two days we only got out of bed to eat, shower and do it all over again. I swear, I was just so caught up in it that I didn't even think about time passing or people being worried about me."

Bonnie was shaking her head, slowly. I could tell by the look on her face that she didn't believe what I was saying, but she didn't say that outright. Instead, she said, "Why not tell us this before? I mean, you're over 21 and single, and so is he, I assume...so why hide it?"

Again, I went for the lie.

"His roommate, is a woman. They have a baby together. He's working on leaving, but it's complicated. I promised him I wouldn't tell, anyone."

My friends exchanged another glance and then Marta crossed her skinny little arms again and sat back into the chair with her lips pursed.

Bonnie looked like she was trying to process it all, or maybe she just didn't believe a hot guy like Ridge would want me. "So... this creep is married, with a baby?" Marta said,

"And he let you tell some bizarre story and be embarrassed in front of the cops, us, your parents...most of the island, to protect him?"

"He didn't ask me to lie, and honestly, I did it as much for me as for him. I knew about the girlfriend before I left with him, he was honest with me. I wanted him, so I did this, and then I was ashamed of myself so I lied."

"I don't believe you," Marta said.

"Me neither," Bonnie chimed in.

I know, since I was a big, fat, liar, it wasn't fair, but I did my best to turn it around on them.

"So what don't you believe? That this hot guy wanted me? That any guy wanted me?"

"No! Stop that," Marta said. "Of course he wanted you. You're gorgeous even though you have no idea. That's not what we're saying. It's just, the idea of you being with a man who is cheating is so out of character for you, and the sneaking around, not answering your phone and making up stories. None of that is in character for you."

"I know," I said. "I've always been the good girl. But I have urges like anyone else, and...there was just something about Ridge, I was drawn to him from that first night we met. I've never been that drawn to anyone." At least this part was true. "I thought about him all the time and the highlight of going out, was seeing him. He was so attentive. He told me I was beautiful...I needed all of that, and I got lost in it. I'm truly sorry that I worried everyone, and that I lied. But haven't either of you ever done anything foolish because you were crazy over a man?"

They were quiet for a long time before Bonnie said, "I have, more than once."

"Me too," Marta said. "But I have one more question...two, actually."

I cocked an eyebrow. "Okay?"

"Are you still seeing him?"

"No. I told him I couldn't do it, not unless he takes care of his relationship first. Question two?"

"The jumpiness, nervousness, always looking over your shoulder...what's that about?"

"That has nothing to do with Ridge," I said, trying to think of a story as I went along. "Or maybe, it does. But I'm not afraid of him, or anyone in particular. I guess my conscience is just stronger than I gave it credit for. The guilt is eating away at me...like the Tell-Tale Heart." They weren't avid readers like I was and they both looked at me, blankly.

"Edgar Allan Poe?" Still nothing.

I sighed and said, "It's a book, about a man who commits a grievous sin and then loses his mind over the guilt. Don't worry though, I'm not losing my mind. I'll be okay. I just need some time to work through it."

I stood up and the girls did too. Bonnie suddenly hugged me and then Marta hugged us both and said,

"Please don't think you can't tell us things. We won't judge you."

I truly loved them, and I despised lying to them even more because of it.

They trusted me and that caused an ache in the center of my chest.

I whispered a "Thank you," and hugged them back and then I went back to wondering just how long I was going to wake up every morning with a knot in the pit of my stomach, and fall asleep every night with the face of a man I simultaneously wanted and feared, seared into my brain.

It was Sunday, my day off. I was relaxing at the compound, thinking about going for a run along the beach and just having a peaceful day.

Then my phone rang...and the man on the other end did his best to change all that. I listened carefully to what Ridge was saying, reacting silently to a lot of it, but not speaking a word until he wrapped it all up by saying,

"Grayson, before you say no, please remember everything we've been through together..."

"Oh that's low." Ridge was my hero, my savior, and he knew it. He's a good guy, but he's a self-centered guy and he doesn't hesitate to use what I "owe" him to get what he wants.

"I'm sorry, Gray. You're right, it sucks for me to do that to you. I just can't explain how badly I want this."

"I know you, Ridge. When you want something, you want it badly and you'll do anything to get what you want, including pulling me into this mess. I'm 19, Ridge. I grew up an orphan wolf so all I know about any of that came from you. I've only lived as a human for a year, so I don't know much about that either. If I get expelled from this pack, I won't make it. I have to wonder how much you value our friendship when I think about you putting me in that position."

"I'm sorry," he said, sounding genuinely remorseful.

"Why not ask Chase?"

"Chase will be expected at work tomorrow. I heard Clay say you have this week off, that's what made me think of you."

"Right, that and the fact that I never say no to you. Where will they think I am all week?"

"Running in the woods. You know they don't keep tabs on us on our days off. You don't have to stay all week...just a few days. Just find out if she's thinking about me, or talking about me. Find out if she hates me, or if there might still be a chance....Come on buddy. You're the right color and your eyes are blue...they'll believe you're a dog, a husky or whatever."

"Thanks, it's nice to know I look like a dog."

He growled a little and said, "Okay, never mind. I'm sorry I asked. I have to get back. The police are still combing through the scene and asking questions. I'm so fucking tired. We were here all night Friday, most of the day yesterday and they called us back out first thing this morning. Maybe I just need to sleep. Maybe I'm just not thinking straight." I thought he was finished and then he said, "I just ache for her, Gray. I can't even describe it. It's hard to breathe."

Damn it.

A surge of guilt washed over me. Ridge had never had anyone. He was told to watch me and for years, that's what he did, alone in the woods.

He raised me, he kept me safe, and he never left me to go looking for a mate or a new pack. If Courtney and the other alphas had wanted him and not me when they found us,

Ridge would have refused to go with them, I knew it in my heart.

Now he had a chance to be happy, and I could help him, but I refused because I'm afraid of getting into trouble. I'm not a pup anymore. I guess it was time to start acting like the adult wolf and human I am. "Ridge, wait. I'll go." There was a long pause and I thought maybe he'd already hung up.

Finally he said, "Really?"

"Yeah, I'll do it."

"If you're worried about getting into trouble..."

"I am, but I owe you my life. Being afraid of a little trouble makes me feel like a coward and I don't want to feel that way."

"Thank you, Gray. I promise, if somehow they find out, I'll take all the responsibility." We ended the call and I thought about what he said. I didn't doubt Ridge would step up because that's just who he was. But he and I both knew that's not how it works in the pack. Each man or woman was responsible for his or her own actions. I knew what I was doing could get me into a lot of trouble and if I got caught, the responsibility for making that decision would be on me. Period.

Surga doesn't have any big department stores or chain grocery stores where I could go and discreetly make a purchase.

I was going to have to go straight to the vet's office to do this, and I hated going there. In any other town that wouldn't even be an option on Sunday...but our vet was open seven days a week, and even on holidays.

I walk by the office all the time, but I had only been inside once, with Courtney about six months ago. We had found a cat and honestly, I'd tried to eat it.

Courtney stopped me, reminding me that we were more than animals.

The cat was domesticated and on the blue collar he wore around his neck was a tag that said, "Hank" and an address. She said some child was probably crying herself to sleep at night, looking for her cat.

Courtney grew up human, so she knew more about these things than I did. I wouldn't argue with Courtney even if I thought I knew more, I had too much respect for her than that. Anyways, Courtney and I took the cat to the address but the house was empty.

The neighbor told us they had recently moved. So, Courtney's next stop was the vet's office. She was going to take the cat in, but about that time, baby Christopher began to cry.

The babies were only a few months old at that time and Courtney was breast feeding them. I left her to feed Christopher and I went inside.

The smell of the place was overwhelming for a wolf, or maybe to everyone, I wasn't sure.

All I knew was that there were things in the air that made me cycle from hungry, to aggressive to horny in a matter of seconds.

I could hear the dogs barking out back before I even went inside, and I hated thinking about them being in cages. I know I couldn't survive being caged in.

On the other hand, dogs don't like us usually. They can smell our wolf and it makes most of them aggressive, so I was safer with them in cages I suppose.

Anyways, apparently they have some kind of "chip" they somehow poke into domestic animals and then the vet can scan them, like a grocery item, to find out where they live.

When they scanned him, his old address came up, but

there was a note in the computer about him getting lost and a new address. A little girl got her cat back...so the trip was worth it. Of course that didn't make it any easier to go inside this time.

The bells jangled as I pushed the door open and a lady at the reception desk looked up and smiled. I made myself smile back and hoped my voice wouldn't crack from nerves when I spoke. "Um, yeah. I got a new puppy and I was looking for one of those machines where I could make a tag for him, in case he got lost or something."

"Oh yes, we have one of those," she pointed to the far corner of the waiting room, right next to where a big ass German Shepard sat with his owner. The dog's brown eyes were already on me. His ears were standing straight up and he was growling low in his throat.

"Oh, okay, thank you."

"The best thing to do for the long run would be to bring him in for his vaccinations and have him chipped." I was glad I already knew what that meant. I smiled and nodded and said,

"I intend to, thanks. I'm just on my break from work now, but when I figure out my schedule, I'll call for an appointment."

"Good," she said, smiling brightly. "We can also schedule the neutering at the same time, if you're planning on having him fixed."

Ouch. I felt an ache in my loins. I'm glad wolves don't get domesticated. If they take my balls, they may as well just take the rest of me with them. I had to work hard to force the next smile. I nodded, thanked her again and tried not to hold my crotch protectively as I walked toward the machine.

I heard the German Shepherd growl and her owner say, "Oh hush, Ellie. What's wrong with you? We don't growl at people, it's rude."

I smiled at the lady, that only seemed to piss the dog off more and the hair on her neck and back rose higher, her ears pinned back and she stood up straight on all fours and began to bark. I could tell the lady was doing her best to hold the dog back and I wasn't sure how long she would be able to, since the dog looked like it outweighed her by about fifty pounds.

With a hand that was shaking because I was trying so hard to move fast, I picked the first tag that popped up when I touched the screen. It was shaped like a dog bone.

Next, I put in the name, "Gray." Then the address. It was the address that Ridge had text me, the address of Cheyenne's apartment complex. She lived in apartment 4. I didn't ask him how he knew exactly where she lived and he didn't tell me.

Anyways, on my tags, I just left off the apartment number. I fed money into the slot and waited for the little tag to finish engraving.

The German shepherd was going insane and the lady was sweating. The tag popped out at last and I looked at it and then tucked it into my pocket before walking in a wide circle around the German shepherd and smiling at the receptionist as I passed the window. I let out a breath I'd been holding as soon as I walked out the door.

The island was small, thank goodness, because I walked everywhere I went. The pack has two cars that we're all allowed to use for groceries, business, or appointments.

But I didn't think this would qualify for any of that. My next stop was a little hardware store where I bought a dog collar to put the tag on, and once I had that, I headed toward the address Ridge gave me. It was Saturday, late morning and I wondered what I was supposed to do if she wasn't home. I didn't want to call Ridge again, however, so I decided to wing it. I walked until the buildings of the little town began to disappear behind me.

Once I was in a secluded area, I ducked into some trees and bushes. I slid the tag onto the collar and lay it down on the grass while I stripped off my clothes, and shifted. I left the clothes, but picked the collar up in my teeth and using the back roads that encircled the town, I ran until I was on the other side of the island, rolled in the dirt so that I hopefully looked more like a stray dog than a wolf and then found a comfortable spot underneath the steps that Cheyenne would have to walk up to get to her apartment.

I parked my car and looked up at the apartment building.

It was funny to think that just a few short weeks ago, I was happy.

Now, I just felt like I was going through the motions. I used to be lonely from time to time, I guess everyone gets that way sometimes. But for the most part, I was content and I was sure that when the time was right, I'd meet some nice young man and we'd get married, have a family...you know, normal stuff.

Then, I met Ridge, and now not only could I not stop thinking about him, but I felt guilty for thinking about him. I felt weird, like there was something wrong with me for wanting a man who would take me and hold me captive.

Sometimes, mostly late at night when I was really lonely, I'd start making excuses for him. I'd tell myself that yes, he did take me, but he didn't hurt me. He didn't rape me. He had plenty of opportunity, had he wanted to do anything awful to me, and he didn't.

Then I'd remind myself that he did drug me, and drugging and kidnapping a woman because you "want" them, isn't normal. But Ridge isn't normal, and that white wolf, Courtney, tried to explain to me that Ridge had grown up wild, not quite human, I suppose. So, he thought what he was doing was normal...but was that really an excuse? Am I pathetic for trying to find one for him? I have no idea...but all of it was making me feel as if I was losing my mind.

I sighed and got out of the car. I grabbed my yoga bag from the back seat. Myrna usually does yoga with me on Sunday mornings, but she had a family thing to go to in Bali today.

Bonnie always spent Sundays with her grandmother, so at least today I'd have some time to myself and they wouldn't be around to stare at me like I might break. I crossed the parking lot and was almost to the stairs when the sight of fur caught my eye.

Something white and gray was laying under the stairs. It sort of looked like a dog, but it was bigger and it was really dirty. I stopped, afraid to approach the stairs with him lying underneath it. Was he lying in wait?

The dog lifted his head and looked at me. He didn't look aggressive, at least not in that moment. He was holding something in his teeth. It looked like it might be his collar. I wondered if someone was looking for him. I said a silent prayer that it wouldn't attack me as

I slowly approached it. I've never had a dog, and there aren't that many of them on the island.

Talking in low, sweet tones I said, "Hey guy. What are you doing under there? Where are you supposed to be?"

The dog's eyes were light blue, almost clear. I'd never seen eyes like that before, but they were beautiful. He wasn't growling at me, or making any kind of aggressive moves, so I got a little closer, squat down and put my hand out so that he could smell it. When he did, he opened his mouth and let the collar with the tag on it, fall at my feet. I scratched him under his chin and he lifted it and closed his eyes like he liked it. With the other hand I reached down and picked up the collar. It said his name was Gray and the apartment complex address was imprinted on the tag...but there was no apartment number. "Gray, huh? So, you live here?"

He didn't answer me, of course.

I looked around me. There were fifty apartments in our complex. Only about half of them were occupied, but knocking on 25 doors could still be time consuming. Yet, I couldn't just leave him there. What if he got into the parking lot and got ran over? I would feel horrible.

My eyes fell on apartment number one, the super's apartment. If anyone knew who owned a dog here, it would be him. I stood up and the dog immediately came out from underneath the steps and stood next to me. I smiled and reached down and pet him again. He was so soft. He was big too, now that I saw him on all fours.

He nearly came up to my waist. I didn't know much about dogs, but I thought this one was a husky or a malamute. They were normally arctic dogs and I wondered what the heck he was doing on a tropical island. "Come on Gray, let's see if we can figure out where you belong." The dog wagged his tail and followed me over to the super's apartment. I knocked on Mr. Balik's door. I was still learning about the Balinese. Myrna told me he wasn't really Mr. Balik. His name was Wayan Balik...which meant, "Wayan again." Eldest boys are named Wayan and there are names for second, third and fourth sons. The fifth one starts it all over, and that was Mr. Balik. I snickered at the thought of me calling him "Mr. Again," but the American in me couldn't help it. It was Mr. this or Mrs. That in my world.

Mr. Balik opened the door with a big smile on his face. I had lived there for over six months now, and I never saw him when he wasn't smiling. He was only about five foot tall and his skin was olive colored. His eyes and hair were jet black and no matter what time of day you knocked on his door, he was always perfectly groomed, like he was waiting for company.

"Miss Cheyenne," he said, "How are you?" He enunciated his English words precisely. The accent was still there, but his words were perfect.

I smiled back at him and said, "I'm good, thank you..."

"You have a dog!"

"Well no. I found him, under the stairs. He has this collar," I said, holding it out to Mr. Balik. He squinted at it and I said, "It's the address of the complex but no apartment number. I was hoping you might know who he belongs to?"

He shook his head and looked perplexed. "The only people who had a dog here moved out about two months ago. I don't think they had such a big dog though."

"You never saw their dog?"

He shook his head again. "No. They paid a pet deposit but no, I never saw the dog. I think it was a small dog though, it lived inside."

"I hope they didn't forget him. Maybe he got scared when they were moving and ran off. Do you have any way to reach them?"

"No. No forwarding address."

"Dang. I'm not sure what to do with him. Is there an animal control on the island?"

"No, just the veterinarian. Maybe you could take him there." The dog started nudging my leg, like he was trying to nudge me away from the apartment door. I laughed and said,

"I don't think he likes that idea." I pet him again and he looked up at me and I swear he was smiling. "Mr. Balik, would it be okay if I kept him just for a few days and put up posters to try and find his owner?" The little man laughed and my face was suddenly on fire when he said, "Just like the posters up for you!"

I forced a laugh. "Yeah, like those."

He waved a hand at me and said, "Sure, sure. You're a good tenant. Just make sure he doesn't bite nobody."

"I will. Thank you." He went back inside and I looked at Gray and said, "I guess you're staying with me for a few days." He smiled again and wagged his tail.

I smiled back. Maybe he'd help me with my loneliness.

He followed me up the stairs and as soon as I unlocked the door and opened it, he walked inside, like he owned the place.

I smiled and followed him in, tossing his collar and my keys on the counter. I put my hands on my hips and said, "I have to apologize, I don't know a thing about dogs. Are you hungry?" As if he understood the question, he got excited and ran over to the refrigerator, wagging his tail.

I laughed.

"Okay, let's see what we have here." I opened it and picked out some leftover chicken and pasta. "Myrna made this, it was pretty good. Well, not really, but maybe since you're a dog, you'll like it, huh?" Myrna wasn't the best cook, but she tried and I didn't want to hurt her feelings, so I choked it down. Maybe the dog can help me out there too. I put it in a plastic bowl and set it on the floor. Then I filled another bowl with water and put it on the floor too. Gray sniffed at it, but he didn't take a bite. "I'm sorry. I guess you don't like it either? Tell you what, let me shower and I'll run to the store and get some dog food, okay?"

Again, he didn't answer me. I rubbed his soft head and headed for the bathroom. When he started to follow, I said, "Oh no, Mr. No boys allowed in the bathroom or bedroom. I'll be right back, okay?" I'm not sure why I kept saying okay like I expected him to say it back, but he sat down in the hallway and didn't try to follow me any further.

As I gathered my things for my shower I realized I felt happier already. Maybe I didn't need a man. Maybe all I needed all along was a dog, or a therapist. I laughed out loud and decided that yes, the therapist might be a good idea.

GRAYSON

I waited for the shower to come on and then I shifted. I started to pick up the bowl of chicken and pasta and remembered suddenly that she had a room-mate. It would probably not be good for her to walk in and find a naked man in the kitchen.

I went over and locked the door and then picked up the bowl and stuck it in the microwave. I might look like a dog, and yes, I've been known to eat road kill when times got hard...but, I was human enough these days that I wasn't about to eat cold food out of a bowl on the floor.

That was funny, actually. All I knew about being human, the Pack had taught me over the past year. Ridge helped too...some.

Before times got desperate for our old pack, Ridge was old enough to go into town and hang out with the humans...girls mostly. He had always had a penchant for the human girls.

While the food was heating, I took a glass down out of the cabinet and opened the refrigerator. I'd seen a bottle of wine when she had the fridge open before, it was red wine, it would go nicely with my pasta. I was happy to see it was already opened and I poured myself a glass, it was early in the morning for wine, but I was pretending to be a dog, currently standing naked in a stranger's kitchen, waiting for the food she'd given me cold and on the floor to heat up in the microwave. I deserved a glass of wine, and damn it was good. As soon as the microwave dinged, I took the bowl out, found a fork and went over and sat down at the table with it...like a human.

I eat fast, and that was a good thing since it turned out that Cheyenne showered fast too. I heard the water shut off and shoveled in the last few bites, drank the rest of my wine, rinsed out the glass, put it back in the cabinet and threw the bowl back down on the floor. I shifted just as I heard the bathroom door open.

Seconds later, Cheyenne appeared in the hallway, wrapped up in a towel. She smelled good and her skin was all dewy and fresh looking. She looked at me and smiled and then looked over at my bowl.

"Wow! I guess you just don't like eating in front of people, huh?"

She came over and squat down to pet me. It wasn't my fault that my eyes were level with her cleavage. She had nice cleavage and I was suddenly feeling things I shouldn't be feeling for my best buddy's mate, but she was touching me, and it was hard to put all of that out of my mind. "You're a good boy, aren't you? You're so handsome too." I pulled my head up and closed my eyes. With a satisfied smile on my face I let her pet me underneath my chin. This gig might not be too bad after all.

As soon as I had that thought, I heard a key in the door. I remembered I was supposed to be acting like a dog and I started wagging my tail and ran toward it.

I saw Cheyenne frown and look at the doorknob as it

turned. I wondered if she was trying to figure out if she locked it or not. I had forgotten that, I'd have to be more careful. It opened and a pretty little dark-haired Balinese girl walked in. I rubbed up against her and watched as she looked at me with a shocked look on her face. "What the heck? Where did he come from?"

"Why are you home so soon?"

The little petite brunette growled and said, "My family...I can't deal with them today. I was on the ferry when my sister called me to complain about my mother and as soon as I hung up with her, my mother called to complain about my sister and my father. I told her I was ill and I wasn't going to make it to brunch. As soon as the ferry docked, I got on the return ferry and came home. Your turn now, where did that hairy beast come from?"

"I'm sorry. I was going to text but I didn't want to bother you. Isn't he pretty? His name is Gray." I stuck out my tongue and wagged my tail, waiting for her to say I was pretty. Instead she said,

"He needs to brush his teeth. Whose dog is he?"

Well that was insulting.

I brushed my teeth this morning. It was her chicken and pasta that gave me the bad breath. It wasn't even all that good anyways. It would probably give me heartburn.

"I don't know," Cheyenne said. "I found him downstairs. He has a tag and a collar. It's got this address on it but no apartment number. Mr. Balik says there's no one here with a dog so I'm going to put up posters and see if anyone claims him. I hope you don't mind if he stays here? It'll only be for a few days."

The little dark-haired girl raised an eyebrow and said, "Is he housebroken?" Jeez, insult to injury. Of course I'm house broken.

"I think so," Cheyenne said. "Let me get dressed and I'll

take him out." Take me out? She expects me to go outside like a common animal? I mean, yeah, of course I've gone outside before, most of my life in fact. But that was in the woods, in the wild. I can't just pee on a main street in town.

Cheyenne bent down and rubbed my neck. Her face was close to mine, so I licked it.

She laughed.

"That tickles, and Myrna's right, I'm afraid, you could use a toothbrush...or a mint."

Wow, do they even know I have feelings? I watched Cheyenne go down the hall toward her bedroom. Once she was gone, I turned to look at Myrna and she was frowning at me.

I whined at her and wagged my tail.

She made a face and then walked past me into the kitchen without even so much as a pat on the head. I'm not sure I like this one. I sat down and watched her open the fridge. She pulled out the bottle of wine I'd just sampled and she frowned again and held it up.

Damn, she noticed that some of it was missing. Maybe she'll think Cheyenne drank it. I watched her take down a wine glass and pour the wine into it.

About that time, Cheyenne came out of her room in a pair of jeans and a t-shirt. Her hair was wet still, but she was braiding it as she walked toward us. She was really pretty. I was busy staring at her when Myrna said,

"Did you have company today?"

"Just Gray," she said, giving me a cute little wink. She's an animal lover for sure, that's a check in the pro's category.

"Does Gray drink wine?"

Cheyenne looked confused. "No..." she chuckled. "Why do you ask?"

"Well, I know you don't, and I just opened this bottle last

night. There's more than the one glass I drank gone. I thought maybe you snuck hot guy over here while I was out."

Hot guy? Who's this "hot guy"? Ridge won't like that and I didn't want to be the one to tell him. He has a temper sometimes. "Myrna! I told you, I'm not seeing Ridge again. Maybe we should talk about you drinking wine at ten am."

"Trust me, if I would have made it to brunch, I'd be drinking whiskey. I'm sorry. I don't mean to be in such a foul mood. But my family..." she rolled her eyes and took a drink of the wine. Her phone made a noise and she picked it up off the counter and looked at it. The grumpy look on her pretty face turned into a smile instantly.

"Brett?" Cheyenne said to her friend with a smile.

"Yeah, he wants to take me on a picnic for lunch."

"Awe, that sounds like fun."

"He's so different from every guy I've ever dated," she said. "I keep waiting for the real him to show up, you know?"

"Maybe this is the real him."

Myrna's smile looked sad. "How is it that after everything, you're still not cynical?"

Cheyenne laughed. "Are you kidding? I'm cynical all the time. I'm still shocked that Ridge wanted me."

Myrna's eyes narrowed. "You're too good for him," she said. "Once a cheater, always a cheater." A cheater? What did she mean by that?

"Well, I'm not seeing him again, so it's not even worth talking about."

Cheyenne's emotions changed abruptly.

I could sense it.

The more I was around humans, the more I realized that I was actually better at sensing how they were feeling than most.

Ridge was well aware that I had that ability, and I didn't doubt that was part of why he'd sent me here. I heard in his voice earlier on the phone that he wasn't going to give up on her no matter what anyone said.

The rest of the pack didn't know him the way I do. Ridge has never wanted something as badly as he wanted her.

Cheyenne bent down and rubbed her hand from my head to my tail, I worried once again about how much I enjoyed that.

"You ready to go out and potty, guy?" Suddenly I forgot how good her touch felt and I was annoyed. Go out and potty? She's got to be kidding, right? I looked up at her face and saw that she wasn't.

She stood up and walked over to the door and opened it.

Tapping her thigh she said, "Come on Gray, let's go out and potty! Come on boy." Completely humiliated, I hung my head and followed her out. Ridge was going to owe me big for this. I followed Cheyenne down the steps and to the grassy area out front. She sat down on a wrought iron bench and in a high pitched voice she said, "Go potty guy!" Fat chance. No way was I "going potty" in front of her, on the lawn, in front of an apartment complex, in the middle of town. No way.

"We're going to stay out here until you go. If you go in the house, Myrna will throw us both out on our ear." Damn it.

Ridge is going to owe me big, times a thousand.

BY THE TIME I finally "went potty" behind the building where she couldn't see me humiliate myself, Myrna had left for her picnic. It was getting close to lunch time and I was getting hungry.

Once we were inside, Cheyenne started making herself a turkey sandwich, and suddenly seemed to remember she hadn't given me any food since the pasta that morning.

"Oh poor Gray! What a crappy pet owner I am."

She looked down and I was staring up at her.

I trained my hungry eyes on the turkey sandwich and she smiled and said, "You hungry guy?" In the spirit of humiliating myself, I wagged my tail and panted, with my tongue hanging out the side of my mouth like a cartoon character.

She ruffled the hair on the back of my neck and said, "I'm sorry I didn't get any dog food yet. I will, I promise." My eyes cut back over to the turkey and she said, "I get the feeling you don't mind not having dog food, huh?" With another laugh she tossed a few pieces of the sliced turkey into "my" bowl.

I walked over to sniff it but waited until she turned to finish making her sandwich to wolf it down. When she turned back around and looked at my bowl she said, "Wow, you were hungry. Poor thing. I promise we'll go get some dog food as soon as I finish my lunch."

She sat down at the little kitchen table and I went over and curled up at her feet.

While she ate with her left hand, she rubbed my fur absently with her right she looked like she was deep in thought. I wondered what she was thinking, but didn't have to wonder for long. After a few minutes she said, "You're lucky." I lifted my head to look at her face and she said, "Dogs don't have to worry about dating, or falling in love, or getting married. It's messy business."

She took another bite of her sandwich.

It looked delicious.

"I'm still young," she went on, "I have a lot of time left to date and to find that special someone. But I can't help but wonder if it's going to hurt every time it doesn't work out. Don't tell anyone," She said to me, the dog, even lowering her voice to a whisper, "I didn't have my first date until I was 19 years old and in college. I didn't even have sex until I was almost 21."

Without even thinking about it, my ears perked up and I sat up straighter. I'd never had a girl tell me about her sex life before.

She was looking at me and she laughed and said, "Typical man. I mention sex and all of a sudden, you're interested."

She wasn't mad though. She petted me again and went on, "I discovered early on that sex was the only interest they had in me. Why is that, Gray? I think I'm a nice person, smart, kind of interesting if someone took the time to listen to what I have to say." I thought she was smart and interesting. I let out a little bark and she smiled sweetly and said, "You're interested, aren't you? You're a good boy. Such a good listener."

I shamelessly liked it when she called me a good boy.

She let her hand swing down in front of me with half the turkey sandwich clutched against her palm. "You want the rest, boy?"

I took it, in one bite. If anyone were to judge me for it, I might just eat them too.

"I have a secret. I think I can tell you," she said, "You won't tell anyone else, right?"

I barked again and she gave me another beautiful little laugh, I liked the sound of her being happy...maybe too much.

"I have a huge crush on a crazy man. At first, I thought it was just because he was hot, really hot. But then he kidnapped me, told me some crazy things...and despite all of that, I still ache to see him. Do you think I'm just lonely, boy? Maybe I've made up this fantasy in my head that I can "fix" this guy?"

I barked again and she looked sad and said, "I'm not sure there's any "fixing" for what's wrong with this guy. I don't know, maybe there's nothing wrong with him and I'm being judgmental. Everyone has their quirks, right? Everyone grows up in a certain culture, believing certain things that the rest of us don't understand or believe...maybe that's all it is with Ridge. He grew up in a whole different place." She laughed, but that time it wasn't a happy place.

"The problem is, I guess, that even though I saw a glimpse of that place with my own two eyes...my brain still doesn't want to believe it. I'd almost rather believe he's a liar, rather than a..." she laughed again and that time she sounded like she might cry.

I hoped she didn't cry. I would have no idea what to do with a crying woman.

"I can't even say it." She sighed and stood up. I stood up too and rubbed my fur against her leg. Smiling down at me she said, "Thanks for listening, boy. I guess we should go put up some posters and while we're out, we'll get you some dog food, and maybe some treats."

She sounded excited about that. I couldn't imagine how I was going to choke down dog food, or God forbid, "Treats." I also couldn't imagine how I was going to tell Ridge she still had a huge "crush" on him, when I was crushing on her myself.

CHASE

I didn't know what Ridge was up to, but I could tell he was up to something, and it would probably end with him in trouble and maybe poor Grayson too.

Ridge and the alphas finally got back from the crime scene sight late on Sunday afternoon. I had guard duty on the compound all day so as I was making my rounds, I saw how exhausted they all were.

They all seemed to be interested in nothing but food, showers and bed. I'm not sure what, if anything they'd found out about the dead men yet, but they had spent the better part of two days going back and forth out there with the detectives that came out from Bali.

When I passed by Ridge and Grayson's little cabin, Ridge was on the phone. He was inside, but his window was open and it really wasn't my fault that wolves have great hearing.

We all know that, so if he wanted to keep things under wraps, he should lower his voice. I may have stopped when I realized what he was talking about and I may have stood upwind so he couldn't smell me there, hiding and eaves-dropping.

But I was glad I did because maybe I can waylay whatever crazy plans he had now, before he dragged poor Grayson into his mess.

Grayson was so naive and Ridge was his hero. He'd follow him blindly into a fire if he thought Ridge needed him, and sometimes I thought Ridge took advantage of that.

"Hey Gray. I guess you can't carry your phone around on this assignment. I hope you hid it in a safe place. Call me when you get this message. I'm anxious to find out if you heard anything about me...does she hate me, or do you think there's a chance for me? Have you seen any signs of her dating anyone else or anyone else sniffing around, interested? Call me, buddy, please."

Somehow he sent Grayson in to get information from Cheyenne, but how?

Who was he posing as?

I almost went over and knocked on his door and asked him, but I thought hearing it from him would make me complicit.

If I just went on a little investigative excursion of my own, and happened to find something out...well, I couldn't be blamed for that in the end, could I? I looked at the time on my phone.

Hansel, a young wolf that the pack picked up before they left Afghanistan, was supposed to relieve me and take over the post for the rest of the evening in five minutes.

Maybe once he did, I'd take a walk...or more like a run, into town. Sadly, as much as I was curious about what Ridge was up to, I was even more interested in seeing Cheyenne again. I'd never admit that to Ridge.

He was sure she's his mate.

I have no idea what it's supposed to feel like when you meet your mate. I always just assumed that like Ridge, I would just know. What I knew about Cheyenne was that I was drawn to her in a different way than I'd ever been drawn to a woman, wolf or human. I've had her on my mind a lot even before the cabin.

Seeing her in the bar, talking and laughing with Ridge used to cause a little ache in my heart. I would never try to compete with Ridge. He was my best friend, my brother almost, and even if I was disloyal enough to try and compete, Ridge is much better looking than me.

He's bigger and stronger, and I know that he's smarter. No woman would want me, when Ridge was one of her choices. But it wouldn't hurt to look at her, right?

I liked looking at her. I liked her smile and the way her pretty dark eyes lit up when she laughed.

"Hey!" I jumped, startled at the sound of Hansel's voice.

"Hey."

"You were like a million miles away. What were you thinking about?" I felt my face go hot. I'm a terrible liar.

"Lunch," I said.

Hansel laughed. "Yeah? Maybe dinner with a beautiful she wolf."

I rolled my eyes and said, "Unfortunately those are in short supply around here."

Hansel nodded and said, "I say we go back to the old ways, the mating rituals and all that. We could find a few willing human women I bet. It would be kind of fun, to fight for them, don't you think?"

I laughed.

"Yeah, but good luck convincing our human alphas of that." Hanson, like Ridge, Grayson and I, grew up wild.

In the days when our parents were all alive, a female, be she wolf or human, was up for grabs by any UN-mated wolf in the pack.

Even if one wolf claimed her first, the rest of the pack had the right to fight for her. The strongest in the pack always ended up mated first, of course. Courtney and her mates didn't like that idea, mostly because the female wasn't given much of a choice. She was simply taken, fought over, and kept. I can see both sides, I guess. I thought about Cheyenne again and I knew deep down that I wouldn't mind having a shot at her.

But then again, there was no way I could beat Ridge in a fight, so I'm screwed either way.

"Hey, I'm going to take off. I think I'll go into town and grab some dinner, and a beer."

"Alright brother, stay out of trouble."

I winked at him and said, "I'll try, but you know how the women get when they see me." I could still hear his laughter when I was going through the gates of the compound. Punk.

* * *

I WALKED into town and I did get something to eat.

I had a beer and looked at the pretty girls in the bar, thinking about maybe trying to talk to one.

Ridge was usually my wing man when we went out.

Honestly most of the women that did talk to me, did so because they were trying to get close to my "hot" friend. Sometimes they ended up agreeing to go out with me, but only after they made sure they'd have no chance with Ridge. Some days I was glad to get his leftovers, and other days it simply pissed me off, and made me feel pathetic.

I'd gone into the bar, thinking about trying it on my own, but the longer I sat there and looked around, the more I thought about Cheyenne. I told myself I was just really inter-ested in what Ridge and Grayson were up to...but I couldn't deny that I wanted to see her again. I finished my beer and left the bar. I walked down main street and wished I knew where she lived. I remembered her telling Grayson she lived in an "apartment" and I knew there were only two apartment complexes on the island. There was one at each end of town.

As I started walking towards one of them, I told myself I was being ridiculous. What was I going to do, knock on fifty doors? And if she answered one, what would I do then? I called myself an idiot, but kept walking.

The walk took me about fifteen minutes and by the time I turned the corner where the apartment complex was, the sun was going down.

There was a light breeze blowing and I caught the whiff of a wolf blowing in on it. I stopped and listened but all I could hear was the sound of a woman's voice coming from maybe fifty yards away and a dog barking. I went in the direction of the voice, the dog and the smell of the wolf that was growing stronger, when suddenly I saw him.

It was Grayson, and if I didn't know better, he was acting like a damned dog. He was chasing a ball that the woman on the bench had thrown for him. I watched him pick it up in his mouth, turn and run toward her. I realized the "her" was Cheyenne, just about the time Gray caught my smell, dropped the ball and looked over in my direction. I shook my head at him. As long as he was making eye contact with me, I was able to communicate with him in my head.

"What the hell are you doing?"

"Go away," was his response.

"Gray? What's wrong?" Cheyenne got to her feet and was looking around. She looked right at me, but I was standing in the shadows and her human eyes weren't able to make me out. "What's wrong, boy?"

"I'll be damned. She thinks you're a dog? How does she know your name?"

"I mean it Chase. Go," he said. No way in hell was I going away now. I had to know what was going on. I put my hands in my pockets, braced myself for Cheyenne being pissed and

began to stroll across the street. I was about halfway across when my "friend" began to bark and growl at me, viciously.

"Stop it. What are you doing?"

"I told you to go away. Don't make me bite you."

"It's okay boy," Cheyenne said to Grayson, rubbing his fur on the back of his neck. She looked at me then, not taking her hand off of him and said, "I'm sorry. I don't think he'll bite." I stepped out of the shadows then and her expression changed. It turned angry and she said, "Chase? What are you doing here? I might let him bite you after all." Grayson began to bark and growl again. I swear I'm going to kick that pup's ass first chance I get.

"Cheyenne, I was just taking a walk. I didn't know you were here."

"Right. Did Ridge send you?"

I looked at the dog and said, "No. I promise. He didn't send me." Grayson snarled at me.

"My dog doesn't like you. They say dogs have good instincts."

"That mutt is your dog?" I got another growl, this one deeper in his throat than the last.

"He's not a mutt," she said. "And yes...I mean no. I found him. He's mine for now until I find his owners. Anyways, I'm not supposed to be talking to you, remember?"

"Nope," I said. "Courtney never said you couldn't talk to me. It was all Ridge. I didn't kidnap you, Cheyenne."

"You didn't help me either."

"I'm sorry about that. My relationship with Ridge is...complicated."

"Whatever it is, I'm not really interested," she said. Funny thing was, she did look interested, at least in hearing about Ridge. I could feel her body temperature going up and her heart rate increasing when she said his name. She was still stroking Gray as we talked. I didn't like that, of course I did kind of think it was funny that she believed he was an ordinary dog.

"Okay, we won't talk about Ridge," I said. "But maybe you and I could start over."

"Why?" she said, folding her arms. I took a step toward her and Grayson stepped in between me and her and growled. I frowned at him and thought about kicking him out of my way, but I figured that wouldn't go over well with Cheyenne.

"I just feel bad for everything, and I like you. What would it hurt, to just get to know me?"

"Chase...you and I starting over would just be...impossible. What I know about you, and Ridge and... your "people." It would just be too much for me to forget."

"So don't forget it, but don't hold it against me either. I can't help what I am, any more than you can help being female, or Caucasian. Friends don't have to be exactly the same, right? I mean, don't you have friends that aren't female, or Caucasian?"

She rolled her eyes. "Of course. But what I don't have are friends who are wolves."

I looked down at Grayson and with a smug smile in his direction I said, "You seem to like the dog. Wolves aren't much different, just bigger, stronger and better looking." Grayson started to lunge at me but Cheyenne had her fingers linked through his collar and pulled him back. He had a collar. I was cracking up inside over that. Damn, the boy must really worship Ridge to have agreed to this.

"He really doesn't like you," she said, again.

In Grayson's head I said, *If you're really thinking of attacking me, I'll have to shift and defend myself. You think she'll want anything to do with either of us then?* Gray stopped barking, but the low rumble in his throat remained. I looked at Cheyenne and smiled and said, "It's the wolf thing. He can smell me. We're okay though, aren't we boy?" Gray stopped growling as I squat down in front of him. "That's right boy, it's okay. Who's a good boy?" I rubbed the back of his neck and he made eye contact with me. In my head I heard him say,

"If she wasn't watching right now, I'd bite your hand off." I laughed in my head and said, "See, he's a submissive little thing, all calmed down."

"You're an asshole."

I laughed again and then I looked up at Cheyenne and said, "How about I buy you a cup of coffee?"

"I don't know..."

I looked as non-threatening as I could and said, "Please. Public place where they make the coffee with the lids on, you can pick it up yourself off the counter and I won't touch it? I'm a nice guy and I don't want anything from you, just a friend."

Grayson growled again.

He was going to tell Ridge everything and I was probably going to have to fight my best friend...and lose. But once I laid eyes on her tonight, I couldn't help myself. I suddenly really did want to know everything about her, and I wanted to spend time looking into her deep brown eyes while I found it all out.

"Okay," she said at last. "Let me put Gray away." Grayson barked and took a step back. Cheyenne smiled at him, got down on her knees and put her hands on either side of his face. She fluffed his fir and then kissed him on the tip of his nose. "It's okay boy. I won't be long."

"Ridge is going to kick your ass," Grayson said as she led him over to the stairs. I laughed and said,

"Yeah, probably. But while you're licking your dog bowl and he's stuck on the compound, which one of us is having coffee with Cheyenne?"

I was so tired, but I couldn't sleep.

Maybe because even though I'd been exhausted for two days, it was only just after sundown, or maybe it was my thoughts of Cheyenne driving me crazy.

She was on my mind all day, every day, no matter who I was with or what I was doing. And now, as I waited for Grayson to report in, I was worried that something had gone wrong and he'd blown it for me, completely. I finally got out of bed, deciding I would shift and go for a run. Just as I slipped off my pajama pants, my phone rang. I didn't recognize the number, but it was local.

"Gray?"

"Yeah, it's me."

"Whose phone are you using?"

"House phone. I couldn't very well walk in here with mine in my mouth."

"True. How's it going?"

"Well, it was going good, for a while."

"What's that mean? What happened?"

"Chase happened."

"Chase? What the hell? What did he do?" I listened as Gray told me about Chase showing up and talking Cheyenne into going out for coffee. The anger that was slithering through my veins was hot, and as it grew, I almost forgot it was my best friend that we were talking about. Maybe he had a plan to help me. That has to be what it is...it had to be...When Gray finished, I said, "Where did they go?"

"No clue. I shifted as soon as she left and looked out the door. I saw them walking west across the street and then they disappeared behind the buildings."

"Why didn't you follow them?"

"You're kidding, right? What if her roommate comes home and tells her I wasn't still inside the locked apartment when she got here? You want her to believe I'm a dog, I have to act like one."

"Shit. What the hell is he up to?"

"Ridge, I don't want to cause trouble..."

"What Gray, just say it."

"I smelled Chase when he was close to her. He's aroused by her, Ridge. Chase wants her too."

"No. You have to be wrong about that. Chase has never gone after any woman I wanted, wolf or human." Not that we'd had many she-wolves to go after. There had been one or two passing through and that was it. But I'd taken plenty of human women back to their place at the end of a night at the club, and Chase was always content to take the ones I didn't want. No way was I going to believe he'd choose the one he knew I wanted to mark as my own to go after.

"I don't think I'm wrong, Ridge."

"Has she said anything about me, Gray?" He hesitated, for a long time. I thought he was going to tell me there was no hope, that she hated me. Instead he said,

"Yeah. She is still interested. She's just scared."

Relief washed over me. As long as she wanted me, there was hope. "Well then, I have to find a way to ease her mind."

"Ridge..." He hesitated again.

"What Gray? What are you trying so hard not to tell me?" I knew this kid since he was a pup sucking on his mama's teat. There was something on his mind.

"I just wanted to tell you, Cheyenne is a good choice. I like her." I heard something in his voice that said he more than just "liked" her. What the hell was going on? My two best friends were feeling things for my mate? Hanson might be right and we just might have to go back to the old ways. Sadly, I wouldn't want to beat up either one of my friends, but I hoped that no one made any mistake that if it came to that, I could...easily.

I took a deep breath and said, "Thanks Gray. Stay put. I'm going to see if I can find them, and talk some sense into Chase." Gray started to say something else. I didn't want to hear a lecture on how pissed Courtney or the other alphas would be. I wanted Cheyenne, too badly to let anything, or anyone get in my way.

* * *

I STARTED to leave the compound and then I decided I wasn't going to sneak around any longer. If I was ready to man up and go claim my mate, I had to man up first to my alphas.

I walked over to their cabin, took a deep breath and knocked on the door. Will pulled it open. He was dressed in a pair of flannel pajama pants and no shirt.

Since they weren't in the military any longer, most of them had let their hair grow out. Clay didn't let his get too long, just not military short.

Manny's was down to his shoulders, Titan kept his as sharp as it had been in the army, and then there was Will. His hair was down to his shoulders. He'd gotten it braided into Dread locks somewhere on the main island and he had a wild beard.

But if I had to pick my favorite of Courtney's four mates, it would be Will.

He was the most easy-going and laid back of them all, and I was slightly relieved that he'd been the one to answer the door.

"Ridge. What's up?"

"Hey Will. I'm sorry to bother you. Can we talk for a minute?"

"Sure. Let me grab my shirt, I'll be right out." He left me standing on the porch and went inside. He was back quickly with a shirt and slippers on. He lit a cigarette and offered me one.

"No thanks. Will, I have a problem. I don't know what to do about it. I want to do things the right way, and I want to respect my alphas..."

"This is about the girl?"

"Yes. I can't stop thinking about her, Will. How can I just walk away when I know she's my mate?"

Will gave me a sympathetic look and said, "You know, if you'd gone about this the right way in the first place, none of us would have asked you to walk away from her."

"I know, and I'm sorry about what I did. I can't explain it, but it's in my DNA, Will...the old ways. Plus, it's what I grew up with. I know that you and Courtney and the others have your own set of rules and I am doing my level best to respect those rules, I promise you, I am... but I feel like this is killing me."

"Even if I was able to put in a word for you, how do you know the girl would still want anything to do with you...or that we could trust her not to rally the islanders to get us thrown out of here."

"She's had three weeks, Will. If she was going to expose us, she's had ample time to do that."

"You don't think her fear of Courtney's warning had anything to do with her not saying anything?"

"I don't know, maybe. But, if she really wanted to give us up, she could have done it and just asked for protection from the police or something...I don't think she wants to. As far as her wanting me, she still does. Please don't ask me how I know that, but I do. If I have to live on this small island with her, you know I'll eventually run into her again and what if that happens after she settles for someone else? I would like to promise you I could control myself, but I don't think I can do that either."

Will sighed. "All I can tell you, Ridge, is that I'll talk to the others. I can't promise anything though. Exactly how are you proposing to go about it this time?"

"I'll start over. I'll do it right. I'll take her out and court her just like the humans do...whatever I have to do, Will. I just have to see her."

Will nodded. He understood.

I see how much he loves Courtney, and the others. They all loved her so much they were willing to share their lives with her, and their children. I don't think I could do that, but I don't judge them for it. That was all I wanted, a chance to not be judged for who I chose as a mate. I had to have Cheyenne...one way or the other.

* * *

WILL TOLD me to go home and wait for him to confer with the others. It was hard, especially knowing Cheyenne was out with Chase...but, I did it.

I paced.

I drank a beer.

I paced again.

I drank another beer.

When the knock finally came at my door, I'd been so distracted I hadn't even heard or smelled anyone approaching. I ripped it open and found Chase on my doorstep.

"You," I said, through gritted teeth.

"Calm down," he said. "I'm sure you've talked to Gray. All we did was talk and have a cup of coffee together."

"Why?"

"Can I come in?"

"No. Why were you with Cheyenne?"

"Never mind. If you're not going to be reasonable..." He turned and started to leave. I was usually the dominant one between Chase and I. His sudden...assertiveness surprised me.

"Fine. Come in."

He smiled and brushed past me. He wrinkled his nose once he was inside and said, "Did you get a dog?"

"Shut the fuck up. Tell me why you were with my mate."

He raised his eyebrows. "Your mate, huh? Are you sure she's your mate Ridge? I mean, you've been with a lot of women, human women...you sure you're not just bored with the easy ones and looking to go after a challenge?"

"Screw you, Chase. Of course I'm sure. I'm so sure that I went to Will tonight and told him, I have to have her." Chase's eyes widened at that. I was beginning to worry that Grayson was right and maybe Chase was interested in Cheyenne the same way I was.

"What did he say?"

"He's going to get back to me. Now tell me what you and Cheyenne talked about."

"Got another beer?" he asked, as he strolled over to my refrigerator. He was suddenly so confident. Where did this version of my friend come from? He got his beer and sat down at my table and twisted off the top. I was trying to keep myself in check, but I was growing more annoyed by the minute. Finally, after taking a long swig of his beer he said, "We talked about us."

"Us? You and her?" That anger was beginning to sizzle in my blood again.

"No. Us...wolves."

My pulse quickened. "You spoke to her about us?"

"Come on man, she saw you and me and Courtney shift...hell, she's seen me naked." I clenched my fists at my sides. He looked at my hands but ignored them as he went on. "She wanted to know more about us, how we lived."

"What did you tell her?"

"The truth. I told her we basically lived as humans, but that sometimes we got the itch and had to run in the woods, or mountains, or along the ocean, or whatever. She kind of got that. She told me that she likes to walk on the beach when she's feeling stressed."

"So," I said, sitting down in another chair at the table, "It seemed like she would be agreeable to that lifestyle? Our lifestyle?"

"She did, actually...for the most part."

"What do you mean...for the most part?"

"She's human, Ridge. She doesn't want to be claimed. She doesn't want to be marked, or in her words, "owned." She's not going to be the submissive that you want or imagine her to be."

"I don't see her as submissive. All those times we talked at the club, she told me about coming 3000 miles from her home and her family to take this job and make it on her own. I saw the pride in her eyes, and it made her even more beautiful. I'd never want to take her independence from her, Chase. I just want her...worse than I've ever wanted anything."

Chase's features softened and the smug look he'd had since he came in the door faded. "You really think she's your mate, don't you?"

"I know she is, Chase. I need her. She's the other half of me."

"Ridge...there's something I need to tell you..." he was interrupted by a knock on the door, and something told me, it was probably a good thing.

CHEYENNE

"So," I said, as I sat down on the couch next to Gray and pulled his head over to my lap. "I know you didn't seem to like Chase, but I honestly enjoyed myself tonight."

Gray looked up at me and I would swear he had a sneer on his cute little face.

"He's a wolf," I told the dog. "That's probably what confuses you. He's a nice guy though, and he's funny. He seems almost childlike, sweet, kind of innocent..."

Gray growled low in his throat and I raised an eyebrow.

"What's that about?" Just then Myrna opened the front door. Brett was with her. I guess that was what Gray was growling about.

"Hey," she said, "Still have the dog, I see?" Gray got up with his paws on the back of the couch and barked.

"Hey! Stop that. You met Myrna and this is Brett. Be nice." To Myrna I said, "I put up posters, but no calls yet."

"Brett and I rented a movie and picked up Chinese. We're going to watch it and eat in my room. You want some food?" Before I could answer, Gray barked again. I laughed.

99

"No sir, no Chinese for you. You didn't touch your dog food, and I got the good kind for you." Again, I think the dog sneered. He was almost human sometimes, it was a little bit freaky. "I'm good, Myrna, thanks."

Myrna was smiling at me. "You're funny with that dog. You talk to him like he understands what you say."

"I really think he does," I told her.

"Where's he going to sleep? Brett has to leave early in the morning...I don't really like the way he's looking at him."

"Me neither," Brett said. Gray growled again.

"Hey. That's not nice!" I told Gray. "I'll keep him in my room tonight."

They thanked me, took what they needed from the kitchen and went to Myrna's room.

I put on a romantic comedy movie and Gray and I snuggled up to watch it.

As I lay there petting the dog and staring at the movie, I realized something strange. I hadn't thought of Ridge since Chase first showed up.

We had talked, and laughed over coffee. He was really a nice guy, and much less arrogant than his good looking, kidnapper friend. As I ruminated over every word he said and every facial expression he made, I wondered once again if maybe my infatuation with Ridge had simply been my loneliness reaching out for the first opportunity that came along.

I lay there and pondered that until suddenly I woke up, hours later, I assume, cuddled up to a sleeping Gray with some sitcom blaring on the television.

I hated to disturb the warm dog, but I shook him slightly, almost like he was human and said, "Hey guy, we need to go to bed, okay?" He yawned and stretched and got up off the couch. He waited for me to turn things off and then he followed me down the hallway.

When we got to my room, I took my night clothes into the bathroom. I know it was silly, but I was shy about my body...even in front of a dog, I suppose. When I came back, Gray was curled up in the center of the bed.

"Hey! Who said you could sleep on the bed?" He raised his head and looked at me with his blue eyes, pleading. I rolled my own eyes. "Okay fine, but don't hog the covers." He rolled over on his back and put his legs in the air. I laughed and rubbed his belly.

Then I kissed him on the nose and we cuddled up and went back to sleep. I could get used to this dog stuff.

RIDGE

I had a restless night, and almost left the compound a few times, but I talked myself out of it. I told Will I would wait to hear back from them, so I did, but not happily.

I fell asleep once, and had a dream...or a nightmare, that Chase and Cheyenne hooked up. I felt like I wanted to kill someone when I woke up. I did leave my cabin after that, just long enough to walk over near Chase's cabin and make sure...number one, that I could smell him inside and number two that I couldn't smell Cheyenne.

She wasn't there and he was, so I went back home, but I didn't get any sleep. I was on my second pot of coffee when Courtney knocked on my door in the morning.

"Good morning. Can we talk?" she said.

"Please. Come in." I let her inside and offered her a cup of coffee. She declined and we sat down at the table. I was as nervous as a damned cat and the worst part was that I was sure Courtney could smell it.

"So, the guys and I talked last night, at length, about this situation with Cheyenne. First of all, I want to commend you on accepting your punishment for defying the rules, the way that you did. You showed real maturity and class and we appreciate it."

"Thank you."

She nodded and said, "We don't want to keep you from the person you believe you should be with, Ridge. Our concern was always this pack first of all, and humans just don't take kindly to being kidnapped, or having their friends or family kidnapped. That's the reason we set the rules down the way we did. We have to protect this pack above all. But...we talked about Cheyenne, and the fact that she has, as you told Will, had ample opportunity to hurt us in the past three weeks, and she hasn't done that. So, in the end what we decided was that you may see her..." I jumped up to my feet without even thinking about it. It was just that sudden burst of adrenaline I couldn't control it. She smiled and said, "Sit down, please." I sat, reluctantly and she said, "But, you have to do it the right way, Ridge. You have to do it the human way, and if she doesn't want to see you, you'll have to accept that. Do you think you can do that?"

I didn't think I could, but I wasn't going to say anything to screw this up. "Yes. I can and will do that." She wants me. I wasn't worried about that.

"Okay then...don't screw this up, Ridge."

"I won't."

"Remember we're a pack. We're a family. We're a team. If you have any problems, come to us. And... I expect transparency. A hundred percent honesty. Got it?"

"Got it. Thank you, Courtney." She nodded again and said,

"You're welcome. By the way, have you seen Grayson?"

Shit. Transparency? Truth? "Not since yesterday morning." Well, that much was true.

"Weird. He told me he'd keep an eye on the babies today

while I did my shopping. The guys are all busy with projects. Is Chase around?"

"Probably. I haven't seen him yet today." Damn it. If Chase says anything to her about Grayson...but then he'd have to tell on himself. I had to get in touch with Grayson and get him out of there or we all might be in trouble, again.

She stood up and said, "I'll go see if he's around. Jackie loves him." That was true. I always wondered what kind of father I'd be, but I knew Chase was going to make a great one. Grayson was good with the babies too. Courtney never asked me to watch them. They made me nervous and I did the same to them. I walked her to the door, thanked her again and then shot Chase a text that I hoped he read before she got there,

"Don't tell Courtney anything about Grayson, please."

By the time I left the compound half an hour later, he hadn't text me back. He was going to let me wonder, and worry. Jack ass.

* * *

I forgot it was Monday. I had to wait all day for Cheyenne to get home from work. Once it was time, I walked to her apartment complex in record time and stood in front of her front door for what seemed like an hour before I finally worked up my nerve to knock.

I could hear my crazy friend in there barking like an idiot and then I heard someone, not Cheyenne, tell him to shut up.

The door was pulled open by her little friend Myrna, who had a smile on her pretty face, until she saw me. "What do you want? Go ahead and attack, dog." Gray was smirking. Little traitor.

"Is Cheyenne here?"

"No. Go away!" She started to slam the door in my face and I caught it. She pulled it back open and said, "Why are you here? She doesn't want to see you! Go home to your girlfriend."

"My girlfriend?"

"Ridge?" The sound of Cheyenne's voice made my heart speed up. The sight of her made me lose my breath.

"Hi."

"I told him you don't want to see him," Myrna said. "May I let the dog bite him?"

Cheyenne looked like she was trying hard to keep a straight face.

"No Myrna, you may not let the dog bite him. Let him in please." Myrna practically growled and rolled her eyes. I wondered if Cheyenne told her I drugged and kidnapped her.

But what was that girlfriend thing about?

She stepped out of the way and I stepped around her so that her little leg couldn't reach if she wanted to kick me.

Gray was down on his haunches, growling at me. I glared at him and then looked up at Cheyenne and smiled. "Myrna, would you mind giving us a little privacy?" she asked her friend.

She sighed, gave me another dirty look and said, "I'll be in my room until Brett gets here. Call me if you need me."

"I will," Cheyenne said. We watched Myrna go down the hall and then into her room. She slammed the door behind her. Cheyenne looked at me then and said, "I'm sorry. She's unhappy with you."

"I see that," I told her.

Gray was still growling and Cheyenne looked at him and said,"Do you want to go in the room too?" Gray stopped growling immediately and actually rubbed himself up against my leg. I almost threw him off of me. Little jerk. "Thank you," Cheyenne said to him. To me she said, "You can have a seat." I sat down and she sat opposite me. Her scent was driving me crazy. My body was reacting to her and I was scared to death that she was going to see the tent that was rising in the front of my jeans. "So what's up, Ridge? Am I wrong, or did Courtney say we shouldn't see each other again?"

"No, you're not wrong. She said that, but they changed their minds."

"Really? Why?"

"Because I explained to them how I feel about you."

She raised an eyebrow and said, "And how is that?"

"I think you're my mate. I can't stop thinking about you, Cheyenne. You're beautiful, you're smart, you have a great heart..."

She was shaking her head. "Ridge, you don't know me. How could you know any of those things about me...except the beautiful part, and that makes me think you need glasses."

"Wolves have senses that humans don't have, Cheyenne, that's the only way I can explain it. That's why humans need time for dating and what not, and wolves...they just mate. They just know. I can feel your heart. I know it's good. And you are so wrong about your looks. You literally took my breath away just now."

Her face flushed red.

I loved that she was so humble too. She was also nervous, I could smell it. She put her hand out and Gray went right to her.

I watched, almost appalled as he jumped up next to her and cuddled up...on her lap. I could hardly breathe as the shock of him doing that right in front of me started to turn into anger.

I wanted to shift and eat him alive as I watched her stroke his fur...so intimately.

"Cheyenne, about that dog..."

Gray lifted his head and looked at me with those blue eyes of his. I saw him as a pup suddenly and reminded myself that he was the closest thing I had to a brother and I'd asked him to do this. But damn it, I wanted her stroking me, not him.

"Yes?"

"Um...I was just wondering where he came from. You didn't have a dog before, did you?"

"No, but how would you know that?"

"Smell," I said, quickly. "I would have smelled him on you. Anyways, back to us..." She had stopped petting Gray. He whined and she started again. The little bastard.

"There is no "us" Ridge. I'd have to be crazy to want anything to do with a man who would drug and kidnap me."

"But you do...I can sense it, Cheyenne. You still want me. Please give me another chance. Please understand that what I did was not to hurt you. I just didn't know any better. I do now, and I won't do it again, or anything like it. I promised Courtney I'd do this the right way, the human way...and if you didn't want me in the end, I'd accept that."

"So by the human way you mean?"

"Dating. I'll take you out to dinner, to the movies, wherever you want to go. Just please, give me a second chance."

She looked at Gray, like maybe he was going to offer his opinion. He looked at me and inside his head I said, *"What the hell are you doing? I didn't send you here to cozy up to my mate."*

"You sent me here to spy on her, and act like a dog, both of which I'm doing. It's not my fault she likes me." Like Chase, he was much more assertive than he'd ever been before toward me. What was that about? Testosterone?

"Ridge, did you hear me?" I hadn't. I'd been concentrating on chastising Gray.

"No, I'm sorry?"

She cocked an eyebrow and said, "I'll go out with you, on a date." I shot up out of my seat and realized that her eyes were on my crotch. Shit. I sat back down and my face was probably scarlet as I said,

"You have no idea how happy you just made me."

I was panting when Cheyenne walked into the apartment. Ridge told me I forgot about taking care of Jack on Sunday and I felt terrible.

On Tuesday, the fourth day of my vacation, I ran all the way to the compound, showered in my own cabin, brushed my teeth and put on fresh clothes and went to see Courtney.

I made up some bullshit story about meeting some new friends, islanders, who were teaching me how to surf. I don't know why that lie...it just came to me. I apologized profusely and spent the rest of the morning playing with Jackie so she could get some work done. I love the little guy and sometimes I thought about when I was a pup and wondered if little Jack knew how lucky he was to have so many people who loved him.

I had that, but only for a short while. Then, all I had was Ridge until the Pack found us. Ridge was good to me, but it wasn't the same as growing up with a mother and father, or in Jack's case, fathers. I had so much respect for the alphas and how well they handled their relationships with Courtney and Jack. They all adored her and the babies, and unless they fought behind closed doors, they all seemed to love and respect each other as well.

I had lunch with Courtney and the babies and left in plenty of time to get back to Cheyenne's and let myself in with the spare key I'd stolen.

The problem was, as soon as I got into town, I ran into Clay.

Courtney told me he was handling some business in town. I almost literally ran into him coming out of the post office. He was on his way to get a sandwich at the deli and although I'd just eaten with Courtney, I didn't feel like I could tell him no.

So, I went to lunch with Clay and ate, and made small talk...telling him the same lie I'd told his mate about why I hadn't been around all week. Clay didn't seem to be in a hurry and by the time he finally headed back and I was free to go, I had about five minutes before Cheyenne got home from work. I ran all the way, racing up the stairs and then sweating bullets as I shifted and stood there naked, trying to get the key in the door with my shaking hands. I made it, just in the nick of time, but I was still out of breath when she walked in the door. She came straight over to me and knelt down to pet me.

"Hey guy. Why are you panting like that? Are you out of water?" She got up and went over to my bowl. "Nope, you have plenty. I hope you're not sick. You're not sick, are you boy?" She knelt back down and gave me more pets and kisses. I know it's shameless, but I loved it, and the thought of leaving her soon made my heart ache.

Not that I wouldn't love for her to know me as a human man...but, for now, I'd take what I could get. She kissed my nose one last time and said, "I have a date tonight, guy. I guess I better get ready."

A date? Shit. I hadn't heard her and Ridge set up a date

before he left the night before. Just the thought of her, out with him, made me green with envy. I wanted to go on a date with her. I wanted her to "get ready" for me. Damn it.

I wanted Cheyenne, to be my mate...not my doggy owner.

She headed for her room and I trotted after her. As soon as she got there, she shocked me by pulling off her dress. She'd never undressed in front of me before. I told myself to turn away, but she was standing there in front of me in a pair of white panties and a white bra.

They were cotton, nothing fancy...but her body looked gorgeous and I couldn't turn away.

She rifled through her closet, laying out a few outfits and then she ruffled my head and went into the bathroom and closed the door. I heard the shower come on and I went over to the bed to see what she'd chosen to wear.

They were all three dresses. One of them was black and looked kind of slinky. I imagined her in it, got a little too excited and then took the hem of the dress in my teeth and bit down, hard. Once my teeth were through it, I pulled, unraveling the hem.

Proud of myself, I did the same to the red dress next to it. I still had the hem of the tan one between my teeth when Cheyenne stepped back into the room, now wrapped in a towel and looking good enough to eat. I stared at her for several long seconds before I realized she was frowning at me.

"What did you do?" She looked like she was torn between being angry and sad, like she might cry...and suddenly I felt bad.

I let go of her dress and dipped my head down. I went over to her and for the first time since we "met," she pushed me away. "No! I'm mad at you! I'm so angry. Why would you do this?" She went over and looked at the dresses. A small, slow tear ran out of her eye and down her cheek. My chest hurt and I wished I could say I was sorry. I tried to rub against her leg again, and again, she pushed me away.

"Go away!" she scolded. "I'm upset with you." I went over and curled up on the floor in front of the window, ashamed of myself...and scared of the way I was feeling.

She was going to be Ridge's mate soon, and then what? I'd have to live on the compound, seeing her and smelling her and knowing Ridge was touching her, every single day.

What have I done to myself?

I wanted her, worse than I've ever wanted anything in my life.

I was working security on the compound again and just about to make a pass on the front gate when I saw Ridge.

He was clean shaven, his hair was styled with some kind of actual product that smelled like coconuts and he had on what looked like a new shirt and jeans. I knew before I asked, but I had to know for sure.

"Where are you off to?"

He raised an eyebrow and said, "Do you really want to know?"

"You going to see Cheyenne?"

I had heard a rumor on the compound, that Courtney and the other alphas had given him their blessing to see her. I hoped it was just that, a rumor. I know I suck as a best friend. I should want him to be happy, and I do...just not with Cheyenne.

"Yes."

"Ridge..." he put up his palm and stopped me. I was interrupted the last time I tried to tell him how I felt too.

He knew.

He had to.

He just didn't want me to say it out loud. "I want her, Ridge," I blurted out. He looked wounded, like I slapped him in the face.

"Well, you can't have her."

"Really? Aren't you supposed to be doing this the human way? If that's the case, then Cheyenne can date whoever she wants. I might ask her out myself."

He narrowed his eyes at me and said, "You wouldn't dare."

"I had a great time with her at coffee the other night. I think she likes me."

"She's just a nice person. Leave her alone, Chase."

"Let me ask you this. This isn't even about me...directly. But what is your little buddy Grayson doing? Why is he still pretending to be her pet?"

"I don't know. I haven't had a chance to talk to him. You know Gray. He has a big heart. Maybe he is just worried about how upset she'll be if he "runs away".

"Hmm, yeah, I'm sure that's it," I said, sarcastically. I rolled my eyes then and said, "Ridge, he wants her too."

"Bull shit."

"I felt it. I could smell it, the other night. Hell, he almost bit me over taking her out for coffee."

Ridge growled low in his throat and said, "Well, he can't have her either."

I felt defiant, something I'd rarely felt in my life. I like to get along, go with the flow...but in this case, I just didn't believe I could do it.

With a tremor in my voice I said, "That's her decision to make, Ridge, not yours. She's not claimed and neither are we. At this point, everyone is fair game."

I chuckled because I didn't know what else to do.

Wasn't it bad enough that I had to be patient and "court" her like a human being? Now my two best friends also wanted to court her? I honestly felt like I was going to lose my mind. "So by 'fair game' - what does that mean? I mean, what do you plan on doing about it?"

"I'm going to ask her out."

"She'll say no."

Chase smiled at me and I saw that same steely determination in his eyes that I saw in my own when I looked in the mirror.

He was about to give me something I'd never had before...competition.

* * *

I WAS FURIOUS WITH GRAY. I kept telling myself that he was a dog and didn't know any better...but, I'd left my things out the entire time he'd been there and he hadn't chewed up a single thing.

It was just my luck that he'd choose tonight to act out. I dug frantically through my closet, finally settling on a blue and white flowered dress. I didn't care for the way it fit me in the hips, but It was close to time for Ridge to show up and I had nothing else.

I finished fixing my hair, curling it and letting it hang down my back and across my shoulders, and then I spent twice as much time on my make-up as I normally did, at last pronouncing myself as decent as I was going to get, just before I heard his knock on the door. I heard a second knock as I pulled on my shoes, and a third when I went looking for my purse. I guess I shouldn't have been surprised to see Myrna sitting in the living room, idly flipping through a magazine...but I was.

"You're not going to answer the door?" I said, annoyed.

"Oh," she said, in an "oh so casual" voice. "Was someone knocking? I didn't hear them."

"You're a butt," I told her.

She smiled. "I'm sorry honey. You know I just love you and don't want to see you hurt."

I had my hand on the doorknob and I looked over my shoulder and said, "I know, but I'm a big girl and whatever happens, I'll deal with it. I just decided that if I don't at least give this a shot, I was going to wonder what if, forever." Myrna's face softened and she said,

"I hear you. Did he at least get rid of the girlfriend?"

"Yes, they broke up two weeks ago," I lied.

She nodded and then positioned herself in front of the kitchen island, with her arms folded as I went to get the door.

Gray, who was acting out as much as she was, positioned his heavy self in front of the door. "I'm coming, Ridge," I said.

Then I looked down at Gray and said, "What are you doing?" He looked at the door and snarled.

"I told you," I said, thankfully, remembering Myrna was still in the room.

"He's an okay guy...just a little different. I'll be fine." I reached down and pet him and then I pulled open the door.

Ridge was clean shaven and his dark hair had been finger styled and set with gel.

He smelled like a summer day in the forest...and the fitted flannel shirt and jeans he wore showed off what an incredible body he had. I felt every nerve ending in my own body react to the sight of him, and then I wondered if he could smell my lust. When I looked at his face at last, I was sure he could. The look on his face was pleased, but smug.

"Hi," he said. "You look amazing." I didn't, but hearing him say I did made the butterflies in my belly take flight.

"Thank you," I said, "So do you." I glanced over at Myrna and she was rolling her eyes. Gray sat at her feet and his blue eyes looked dark as he glared at Ridge. I hoped he didn't decide to bite him. The day I'd watched Ridge shift, I had seen what a big, powerful animal he was. He could easily maul my little husky. Not that Gray was a little husky in any sense of the word...but Ridge was a giant of a man. A hot, sexy, giant.

"You ready to go?"

I picked up my purse and nodded. I turned to Myrna and said, "Can you let Gray out later, before you go to bed, if I'm not home yet?" Myrna rolled her eyes and nodded. Cheyenne looked down at Gray and said, "You be good boy and go potty when Myrna takes you out, okay? I won't be too late." He whined and in my head I heard him say,

"I'll be good. I'll be waiting, in my spot on the bed." Little asshole.

$\mathcal{M}$y heart was beating wildly, skipping beats here and there, and I could feel my panties, flooding with moisture.

Ridge and I had just gotten back to my apartment after our second date.

He'd packed us a delicious picnic dinner and we'd eaten it under the stars on the beach. He held my hand and we took a long walk, barefoot in the warm sand...and we talked, about everything.

It was a wonderful night, the best I'd had in a very long time. I expected him to make a move on me sexually, but he didn't. He promised me on our first date he would wait until I was ready, and as soon as I was, all I had to do was say the word.

With any other man who looked like Ridge, and made me feel the way he did, I would have ripped both our clothes off on that beach.

But I knew making love to Ridge would be different, in more ways than one. To him making love to me would be "mating," a thing he expected us to do for life. As hard as it was...and it was hard, I had to resist my sexual urges until I was absolutely sure it was what I wanted...forever.

When we got back to my apartment, he walked me up to the door and then for the first time, we kissed. My heart was fluttering like it was trying to take flight and every nerve ending in my body felt alive and exposed.

Ridge put a big hand on the side of my face and brought his lips down to mine. His lips were so warm that they bordered on hot and his kiss was slow at first, just sliding his lips over mine.

His tongue came out then and he licked my lips, outlined them with his saliva, before sliding it into the seam and tangling it up with my tongue. He slid his along mine like he was tasting me and then he began to explore the rest of my mouth, and me his. The kiss grew from soft and sweet to hungry, desperate and erotic.

The muscles of his chest were pressed into me and I could feel them ripple against my breasts. My panties were filled with moisture. I wanted him, so freaking badly...but God help me, I just wasn't sure that I wanted to commit to forever, at least not yet.

I was the one that pulled out of the kiss, gasping for breath. He was smiling down at me, his lips red and swollen from our kiss. God I wanted more. I wanted to taste them again. I wanted to taste all of him. I put my palms against his chest to push him away but for a second I got caught up in the feel of it and I wondered what it would feel like in the flesh...the hot flesh.

I gained control of my senses at last and pushed against him.

He took a step back and smiled again. "I can wait for you, love," he said, "It's okay. I know we'll be together forever. I'll let you decide when that forever begins."

Jesus, it wasn't bad enough how hot he was, or how

strong, or that he'd just taken me on a dream date...now he sounded like a freaking poet.

He was killing me.

"I want..."

What did I want?

I wanted him.

I wanted him to rip off my clothes and ravage me and I wanted to do the same to him.

Ridge was nodding.

"I know my beauty. When you're ready. I'll be here."

He kissed me on the tip of my nose then and said, "Go on inside before I lose my last shred of impulse control."

I smiled up at him and he bent down and kissed my lips one last time before I went inside. I stood there for a second with my back against the door, just trying to get my bearings and waiting for the world to stop spinning.

When I felt strong enough, I went toward my bedroom, practically floating down the hallway on the after effects of that kiss. It was only when I flipped on the light in my bedroom that I realized Gray hadn't come to the door to greet me.

That was when I called to him, whistled, and began to frantically search the apartment. I checked every place that he might be able to hide, twice, before I had to accept that he just wasn't there. I felt like I couldn't catch my breath.

Where could he have gone?

He was there when I left for my date. He'd laid in the center of the bed and watched me get ready.

He seemed a little sulky and I felt bad for leaving him again since I'd only just gotten home from work. I fed him a special treat...leftover steak that Brett and Myrna barbecued the night before, and then I gave him lots of hugs and kisses before I left. I knew I was too attached to him, but every day that went by I felt more like he was really mine than the day before.

I called Myrna, in a panic. "Did you see Gray when you came home after work?"

"I didn't go home after work. Brett picked me up and we went straight to his place for dinner. It's his birthday, I've been here all night."

I heard a loud sob before I realized it was coming out of me. "Oh Myrna! He's gone!"

"How? Was he there when you left?"

"Yes."

"Then he has to be there still...no one has been in the apartment, have they? Does it look like we were robbed or something?" I looked around me then. I'd been searching for Gray but hadn't even thought to really look at things. Nothing looked out of place. I sobbed again.

"The door was locked. Nothing is out of place. He's just gone!"

"I'll come home and help you look."

A surge of guilt assaulted me.

"No. It's Brett's birthday. You two have a good night. I'll look for him...maybe I left the door open and Mr. Balik came by and closed it. I'll check with him."

"You sure?"

"Yeah. I'm sorry to bother you."

"Please. You never bother me. I love you, girl. Good luck with the dog."

I smiled and wiped the tears off my face. "Thanks. Love you too."

I hung up and went to change clothes.

I took off the sun dress I'd worn on my date and put on a pair of sweats and tennis shoes. Then, I found our flashlight and went out to look for him. I stopped by Mr. Balik's apartment first, but he hadn't seen him, or been by our apartment.

Disappointed, I started searching for him around the complex. I walked around the front of the apartment complex with tears streaming down my face, calling his name. I made it to the end of the building and as I turned into the dark, a shadow appeared from between the buildings. I put the flashlight on it and saw that it was a man, a young man...with intense blue eyes.

"I'm sorry," he said. "I didn't mean to startle you." I'm not sure how he knew I was startled. My heart was racing, but I hadn't reacted. Ridge could do that, sense what I was feeling. A chill ran through me. I wasn't afraid of Ridge, but the idea of being face to face with a stranger who could morph into a wolf, while I was alone, in the dark did frighten me.

"It's fine," I said, "Excuse me." I turned and started back around the front of the building where there was light, and someone could hear me scream if it came to that.

I heard him move behind me and I moved faster. Then suddenly he said, "Cheyenne." That stopped me in my tracks. If I was smart, I would have run, but if he was a wolf, and he wanted to assault me, running wouldn't do any good. I thought about just walking away again when he added, "Please don't cry, Cheyenne." My name on his lips a second time did it.

I snapped. I spun around and put the light in his eyes and said, "Who are you and how do you know my name?"

Softly, and in a voice that sounded like he was trying to make it non-threatening he said, "My name is Grayson. I'm a friend of Ridge's. I live at the compound."

"Grayson?" A tickle of fear, or horror, began in my belly and slid around to my spine. It climbed up slowly, touching every nerve transmitter along the way like a set of long, cold fingers. "No," I said, shaking my head from side to side. "No way." I was looking at his eyes. I knew what he was. I knew who he was, but my mind didn't want to accept it.

"Cheyenne, it's okay. It's going to be okay..."

"No!" I screamed at him. "No! You're not him. You're not my Gray!" He was staring at me with those eyes...the blue eyes that belonged to the "dog" I'd fallen in love with. I felt sick and dizzy. This was a sick joke. As I clutched my stomach to keep from vomiting it occurred to me that he said he was a friend of Ridge's. Ridge had seen my Gray multiple times. He had to know! He knew? Oh my God...what kind of twisted animals were they? Was I just one big joke to them all? I thought about the kiss I shared with Ridge just minutes ago and I felt sick again. I had to get out of there. The world was spinning too fast and I wanted to get off.

I turned away and started running, but "Gray" was right beside me, matching me step for step without breaking a sweat. Of course I couldn't outrun him. He was a freaking wolf for crying out loud. "Get away from me!" I screamed.

Gray opened his mouth, but whatever he was going to say was cut off. I saw a flash of fur out of the corner of my eye and suddenly Grayson the human was on his back and a large, black wolf stood on his chest on all fours, snarling at his face.

The strangest thing about it was that Grayson the human, didn't look at all distressed, only pissed.

"Get the fuck off me, Chase."

"Chase? Oh dear God." The wolf stepped off of Grayson's chest and in seconds he transformed into the man I knew as Chase...and he was naked. It wasn't the first time I'd seen him that way. He'd been naked that day at the cabin too.

"What did you do to her? Why was she screaming?" Chase was in Grayson's face. Neither of the men seemed to notice that Chase was naked. I looked around to see if there was anyone else around, but we seemed to be alone. I didn't know whether to be relieved by that, or not.

"I didn't do anything to her," Grayson said.

"Nothing but pretend to be my dog for two weeks and..." I gasped. Chase had seen him too. They were all in on whatever this twisted little game was. "You knew," I said to Chase. You and Ridge both knew he was in my house this whole time. What was he, your spy? You're sick. You're all sick!" I had my hands on both sides of my head, trying to keep it from exploding.

"No," Chase said. "I mean, I knew he was there, but I wasn't spying on you, Cheyenne. I would never do that."

I glared at him and then turned on Grayson and said, "You have nothing to say for yourself? You're sick, perverse! You slept with me! You watched me change my clothes! All the while you pretended to be an innocent pup. Oh my God! You're all twisted," I said, again.

"Dude, you saw her naked?" Chase said. Grayson growled at him. I threw my hands up. I was finished, with all of them. Turning on my heel, I started walking toward the apartment. Chase was suddenly on one side of me, and Grayson on the other.

"Please Cheyenne. I came here for Ridge, before he got the alpha's blessings to see you. But I stayed, because I really liked you, and I didn't know how to explain any of this. But, tonight when you were getting ready to go out with Ridge again, I realized it was just too much. It was too wrong and out of control and I had to do something. I planned on just leaving and not ever telling you. But then I saw you crying, and I felt so bad. I would rather you be angry with me, than heartbroken and looking for a dog that wasn't coming back..."

I stopped and it took them both a few steps to realize it.

When Grayson turned back around I got on my toes and into his face.

Gritting my teeth and practically spitting venom I said,

"You...people, or whatever you are, have been playing with me since day one. I've been kidnapped, lied to, made a fool of, and you say you didn't want to see me heartbroken? Are you kidding? I might be inclined to believe that it was exactly what you all wanted. I don't believe anything that any of you say any longer. I don't want to see any of you, ever again. If you leave me alone, starting this very second, then your creepy little secrets are safe with me. But if I see any of you lurking around me again, ever again, the whole world will know about you, and there will be no place any of you can hide!"

I was so angry and my heart was beating so hard and so fast that my chest felt like it was going to split wide open.

I think if either of them had tried to stop me at that point, werewolves or no, I would have ripped them both apart with my bare hands. I stormed back towards my apartment, only to be stopped again, this time by a brick wall.

"Get away from me! Go away!"

"Cheyenne, it's me. It's Ridge."

I left Cheyenne at her door half an hour earlier after our date. We shared a kiss that was so electric I swear the energy from it could have been used to light up a small city. I was almost to the compound when I realized I didn't just have the picnic basket on my arm, I also had her little sweater she had taken off earlier and I'd insisted on carrying for her. I debated just keeping it until the next time I saw her. I liked the idea of having something with her scent on it.

But I also liked the idea of having an excuse to go back and see her again tonight...and maybe getting another kiss. I was almost there when I smelled the wolves and I started running. I told myself it was probably just Gray. The stupid pup was still pretending to be her dog and I hadn't quite figured out what to do about that yet. But I had another gut feeling that something was really wrong. I was so connected to her on an emotional level that I could actually feel her angst. I almost shifted, but the last thing I wanted to do was scare her. I did that anyways when I met her running too. I thought she saw me. I didn't realize she didn't until she slammed into me and screamed.

She was beating my chest with her fists and I realized she was crying.

"Baby, it's okay, it's me." She drew her leg back and kicked me in the shins.

"Ouch! What the hell?"

"Let go of me! Get away from me!" I smelled my two "friends" before I looked up and saw them coming around the back of the apartment building.

Grayson was in human form and he and Chase both looked guilty...like they needed their asses kicked.

"What the fuck did you do to her?" I had hold of her wrists and was having to hold her back so that she couldn't kick me.

"I told her the truth," Grayson said.

"You're all sick!" she yelled.

"I'm sure you all had plenty of laughs at my expense. But, it's over now. Let go of me and go away or I swear to God I'm telling everyone on this island what you really are."

The rage inside of me was quick. It burned like acid and sliced at everything inside of me.

I let go of Cheyenne and without even checking to see if anyone was around, I shifted. Chase saw it coming and he shifted too, jumping in front of me and Grayson as I lunged at him.

Gray was always a little slow on the uptake, even in the wild.

At that moment however, I was too angry to see him for who he was, a confused pup that I had raised. I saw a challenger, a wolf that was trying to take my mate, and trying to hurt her in the process. I hit Chase first and we rolled in the grass, claws ripping at fur and flesh and teeth gnashing.

It was only seconds later before Gray joined us, obviously

on Chase's "team" trying to subdue me. I was too angry to be subdued. I had Cheyenne. She was mine...I felt it in her kiss, and in less than an hour they had ruined that and they were going to pay for it. I could hear her screaming, but it was just background noise as I slashed and tore at my former friends.

The anger blinded me and all I could smell was the scent of Chase and Gray's fear. They thought I might kill them, and they may have been right...but then suddenly a burst of freezing water hit me right in the face. In shock, I unclenched my jaws and let go of Gray's flesh.

He rolled away and Chase started to come at me, but I saw the stream of water hit him too. It wasn't enough to knock us back physically, but it was cold and shocking.

I followed the water until I saw the source of it. Cheyenne had gotten the hose from the side of the building and turned it on.

It was one of those big hoses the island ordinances made every building have in case of fire, hooked directly to a main water line. She was holding onto it with two hands and the look on her face was pure determination.

Strangely, as I saw her pretty eyes flash in my direction and she turned the hose on me once more, my heart swelled with more love for her than I'd ever felt.

"Are you going to stop this!?" she yelled.

Chase and Gray were already lying in a docile position on the ground. I was the only one still trying to move.

The fight had gone out of me; I wanted to move toward her. I stopped and did the same thing my pack mates had done. I lay down in a submissive pose, just long enough to get her to stop.

She didn't take her eyes off of us as she turned off the hose, but as soon as the water was off and she'd taken her hands off the hose, I shifted.

I could see Gray and Chase doing the same out of the corner of my eye. The scratches and bites all over my body were already healing and I assumed theirs were doing the same.

They'd be much sorer and more bruised than I was, probably for days, but they would heal. Even if Cheyenne hadn't turned the hose on us, I would have stopped before I ripped open anyone's throat. I didn't want to kill my pack mates, my best friends...Only slightly maim them.

As wolf shifters we can heal ourselves quickly, thanks to our incredibly hot metabolism. It's why we live so long.

But there are ways to kill us.

We can be starved to death, dehydrated, stabbed through the heart so the flow of the healing blood is interrupted... that's why as wolves, we go for the throat. Once a wolf's throat is ripped open there's too much blood loss for him to heal properly.

Sometimes he can pull himself together enough to keep breathing for a while, but if it's done right, he'll either die on the spot, or very soon after. Now that the rage had receded, it was quickly replaced by the shame of attacking my friends at all.

"You're insane," Cheyenne said, "All of you." It was at that moment that I realized, though we were all bleeding, Grayson was the one she was approaching.

Although he was no longer her dog, but now a bloody teenager, she was kneeling down next to him, using part of her sweatshirt to stop the blood that was oozing from a wound in his neck. He was staring up at her and I could feel the love pouring out of him, so strongly that it seemed to wash over and dilute the jealousy I was primed to feel at that moment.

I looked over at Chase.

He was watching her too, and I felt his own envy toward

Gray and his admiration for Cheyenne...more than admiration...his connection.

Gray and Chase were connected to Cheyenne, my mate, almost as strongly as I was. Or maybe as strongly, and I just didn't want to see that. Was it possible that she was meant for us all?

I thought about Courtney and the alphas and wished I had asked more questions of them, about how their relationship came about and how they tolerated sharing the love of their life with someone else. I was sure the men's close friendship had something to do with it, maybe everything.

They loved each other as much as they loved Courtney, just in a different way. I never imagined that I would be able to share my mate with anyone else, but in that moment, there was so much warmth and love rippling through the four of us, that I had to wonder.

Maybe it was worth exploring...that was, if we hadn't completely blown it with Cheyenne for good. I looked back at her and Gray and concentrated on her this time.

She definitely felt something for him...but he'd been her pet. Would she feel the same way about him as a man?

She turned her head suddenly to look at me and in a commanding tone that I'd never heard her use she said, "Get him into the apartment. I need to clean up these wounds."

"He's healing..." Chase started.

Cheyenne whipped her head in his direction and it was almost like daggers were shooting out of her chocolate brown eyes. I saw Chase do something I'd never seen before, cower to a female. "We'll get him," he said, struggling to his feet. I got to mine as well, deciding things would be better if I just kept my mouth shut for now.

Chase and I lifted Gray underneath each arm, and the three of us, naked as the day we were born, followed Cheyenne to her apartment.

I was just thinking how glad I was that it was such a quiet place when the door three down from Cheyenne's opened and a middle-aged woman stepped out. Her eyes widened when she saw us and I smelled Cheyenne's anxiety as she said,

"Excuse us Mrs. Garrett. My friends had a little too much to drink tonight."

The woman's eyes looked like saucers as she watched us walk inside and I heard her say, "I wonder what the hell they were drinking," as Cheyenne closed the door.

My poor, beautiful mate would be the talk of her complex by morning, I was sure. But since I still planned on changing her address soon, I wasn't worried. As soon as the door was closed Cheyenne said,

"Go put him on my bed, I'm going to get some bandages and antiseptic."

Neither Chase, Grayson or I thought to argue with her. Her tone left no room for it. We took him into her room and I felt another surge of jealousy when we lay him down and I thought about him being so comfortable there in her house...in her bedroom. He curled up like he owned the bed and I rolled my eyes.

Chase picked up an afghan from the bottom of the bed and threw it over him and Cheyenne yelled from the other room, "There's a rack in my closet with a couple of robes. Put them on!" We looked at each other and Chase was the one that went over and got the robes out.

He had a fuzzy gray one in one hand and was holding out a soft, satin pink one in my direction. I growled at him and he handed over the gray one.

By the time Cheyenne came in, we were covered up. She had a little plastic box in her hands and ignoring Chase and I, she sat on the bed next to Grayson and began taking things out of the box.

First, she took out a bottle of water and I watched in jealous fascination as she slipped her hand underneath his blonde head and pulled it up slightly before pressing the bottle to his lips and saying, "Drink."

Grayson did as he was told.

After she was satisfied he had enough water she wet one of the bandages out of the box and began to delicately dab at his wounds. I was oddly aroused watching her. Her touch was so soft and the look on her face, well, that was even softer.

I felt her feelings for Gray pouring out as she tended to each one of his wounds, even pulling the afghan down to the top of his pelvis to tend to a bit just at the top of his right thigh.

Grayson had his eyes closed, but the little shit was almost smiling. I looked at Chase again, and this time he rolled his eyes.

It seemed to me that Cheyenne spent way too much time on Gray's wounds than she needed to, while Chase and I had wounds of our own that she seemed to be ignoring. When she finished at last, she stood up and finally looked at the two of us. I was shocked when her pretty lips turned up into a smile and she said, "You two look ridiculous."

Chase and I looked at each other again. He was the one in pink satin, I didn't think I looked too bad. "Cheyenne," Chase said, being the first one of us to speak. "I'm sorry, for everything." The smile fell from her lips and she frowned. She looked at me and then back at Chase and said,

"I just don't understand why you picked me. There are plenty of women on this island to mess with, why me?"

"Because," I said, "It's never been about "messing" with you. We have real feelings for you, Cheyenne. I love you."

"Me too," Chase muttered, and then from the bed came Grayson's sleepy,

"And me." I growled at them both and went on,

"The three of us have been strays most of our lives, Cheyenne. Before that, we were raised in the wild, under the old rules. Things were so different, and some of it is not just learned, but in our blood. We're all trying hard to be "normal" humans, but I can't even explain how difficult that is. But we are, Cheyenne, human...for the most part. And I..." I stopped and looked at my stupid friends. "We, care so much about you."

Cheyenne looked at me, then at the two of them and sighed.

"Sit," she told me and Chase as she sat on the bed. Chase and I jockeyed for the spot next to her and just as I was about to growl at him, she threw me a look that stopped me. We finally sat and she said, "If this is not a trick...if you're not just playing with me, then what are my options here...my choices, to keep the three of you from killing each other?" She looked at Gray and said, "And pretending to be my dog." Gray smiled. He still had his eyes closed. "It's not funny!" she scolded, but I could see real affection in her eyes when she looked at him.

"We could..." Chase started, and then stopped.

"We could, what?" Cheyenne said.

"I was just thinking, you know about Courtney and our other alpha's relationship, right?" Chase asked. Cheyenne cocked an eyebrow and nervously Chase went on, "I mean, you might not want all of us, but if you did, they've set a precedent. Maybe there's more than one mate out there for some people. I know how strongly I feel about you. I felt it way back when Ridge first introduced us in the bar. We're not like humans in that we don't have to really get to know someone before we develop our feelings. We feel first...and I've felt for you since day one. I'd be okay with you loving my two best friends too...I mean of course, if you were so inclined."

She raised her other eyebrow. I could feel chaos coming from her, and I couldn't get a read on what she was thinking. She looked at Gray then and said, "Open your eyes, pet." Grayson had another little smile on his face as he pulled his eyes open. She rolled her eyes at him, but again, I saw the affection there. "What's your take on this?"

"I feel the same way as Chase. I knew Ridge wasn't going to like it, but the second you found me downstairs, I knew you were more than just my friend's mate. I would gladly live as your dog forever, just to be close to you." I'm not sure, but I think her eyes filled with tears when Gray uttered those words. Little shit. She turned those watery, beautiful eyes on me then and said,

"And you?" Cheyenne finally turned to me.

"I am head over heels in love with you, Cheyenne. I have known from the second I saw you that we belonged together. I want you more than I've ever wanted anything, or anyone. I'm not good at sharing," Chase and Gray both snorted and I said, "Shut up, it's my turn." Cheyenne bit her bottom lip, like she was hiding another smile and I went on, "I hate to share. I'm selfish and arrogant. I know I'm stronger and better looking..." the guys snorted again, but this time Cheyenne let out a little laugh too. Slightly hurt, I went on. "Women want me. I expected you to just want me. I was surprised and confused and hurt when I realized that you also felt something for my mates. But like the dog there, I'd be more than willing to change my life and my beliefs for the chance to be with you. I'll share with these idiots if it means having you."

She was quiet for a long time. The sound of the clock ticking in the living room and our breathing was the only sounds in the apartment for too long. My imagination was running wild with all the possibilities, and I was so nervous that none of them were good. At last she said, "I have a lot of questions."

"Ask, we'll answer them," I said.

She shook her head and said, "No. I want to talk to Courtney."

Chase, Grayson and I looked at each other. I was sure they were all thinking the same thing as I was.

Courtney wasn't happy with any of us right now. It was possible, and highly likely, that she'd tell Cheyenne to run for the hills.

CHEYENNE

TWO MONTHS LATER

I knocked on Courtney's door.

She yelled at me to come in, and I stepped into the cabin, not for the first time witnessing the beautiful chaos that was her life, and would soon be mine.

Never in a million years would I have imagined that I'd meet a wolf-shifter, or even that they existed. Never in a billion years could I have imagined that I would fall in love with not one, but three of them, and never in a trillion years could I have wrapped my head around what was about to happen today.

But this was the choice I'd made and as nervous as I was about it, I was a thousand times more excited. I'd spent a lot of time with Courtney, her babies and her mates over the past two months and I'd witnessed nothing but pure love and happiness.

Of course the men sometimes bickered and the cabin wasn't always neat and clean and sometimes no one could seem to figure out what the babies wanted. Their phones were always ringing thanks to their security business and they'd just wrapped up a huge case where they were responsible for catching a ring of people that were committing insurance fraud and using the money to fund a drug organization.

Four men had been killed...drug dealers, and Ridge had been one of the packs that had found them. I'd watched him for the past few months too, go from my sexy mate, to a serious member of the pack. I'd heard him take charge in a professional way in phone calls with the police in Bali about the case, and I'd heard him take phone calls from one of his alphas where he was almost submissive.

I'd seen him in 3-D was the way I liked to look at it, from arrogant, sexy man, to glorious beast, to a docile servant...and a sweet, kind, loving mate, and even a protective, caring best friend. I knew from the moment I saw him that I was attracted to him.

I knew then, that I loved him.

Then there was Chase. He was the one I could talk to, the one that made me laugh away my problems.

At first, I thought I was confusing my need for a real friend with attraction, but the more time I spent with him, the more I began to see him not just as my friend, but as a desirable man.

Chase wasn't good-looking in the traditional sense, I suppose. He was shorter than Ridge, and not nearly as muscular. He had dull brown hair and hazel eyes and he wasn't ugly, just average...at first. But the more I got to know him, and the more I saw him in different situations, the more attractive he became to me. For one thing, his relationship with the triplets was one of the most heartwarming things I've ever experienced.

He loved those babies like they were his own, and other than their own parents, there was no one they loved more. Chase got this light in his hazel eyes that turned them almost bright green when he looked at them...and that same light was there when he looked at me. I honestly believe Chase would have been the one to walk away first, just to make me happy, had I wanted that...but when I looked deep inside my heart, I knew that wasn't what I wanted. I wanted Chase as much as I wanted Ridge.

I just loved them both differently and for different reasons.

Then there was Grayson. The other guys still tease him about being my "pet," and maybe that's true. Of all three of them, I liked Gray the best.

That's not to say I loved him more, because I didn't. I just felt more comfortable around him, like he's the one that has truly seen the real me, stripped down, bare...and I don't mean naked, although he'd seen that first too. I mean that people are real with their pets, no pretense.

Gray had seen all of that, and he still loved me. He was young, but only two years younger than me. He still had some growing up to do, but so did I. He was definitely beautiful to look at.

As a human with those incredible blue eyes and jet-black hair, the sight of him sometimes sent a chill through me that settled in my core and leaked out into my panties.

I'd chosen all three after spending a lot of time talking to Courtney. There was no pressure to choose any of them, or all of them.

She was just honest with me about her life with her mates, the good and the bad, and she let me see them all at their best and worst. I'd still chosen all three...and today would be the day that I would mate with them, together.

"Hey," Courtney said to me, handing Jackie to Will and saying, "Okay guys, we need the house. It's a no male zone for a while." There were a few grumbles but each one of her mates ultimately kissed her on the cheek and left the cabin. It looked like a tornado had touched down in their living room and she put her hands on her hips and sighed as she looked around and said, "You sure you want to do this?" I laughed.

"Maybe I'll train mine to clean up after themselves." She was the one that laughed then.

"Yeah, good luck with that. It smells like a wet dog in here. I can't even train Will to leave his boots outside the door. But anyways, I'm so excited for you. Are you really ready for this?"

By that, I knew she meant the mating ceremony. I was given many choices about how I wanted to do this, and I chose the "old way" that all three of my men seemed to be so connected to.

None of us had made love yet...that had been incredibly hard. I'd shared kisses and sweet, sexy touches with them all, and I was dying some nights when I had to go home, but I had a feeling it would all be worth it...tonight.

I nodded at Courtney. "I'm sure. I'm ready."

"So your roommate believes your moving in with Ridge?"

"Yes. She's still not happy about it. He's tried so hard to win her over, but she's a tough nut to crack. My other friend, Bonnie...she likes him now."

"Good. I don't want to see you lose your friends and your own identity. It's important for you to hang onto that."

I nodded. I was keeping my job, despite my "mates" objections. They had their jobs, and I wanted mine, at least for now, until children came in the picture and then you never know. "I believe that too," I told her.

"Let's get you ready then."

For the next two hours, Courtney helped me get ready for my big day. I had a new dress, it was off white with a lot of lace and it was fitted to the curves I'd grown up hating, but my mates seem to love. I wore my dark hair down my back and Courtney helped me curl the ends and she'd made me a wreath out of baby's breath to wear around my head.

My make-up was flawless and I wore little satin slippers on my feet. I'd never felt more beautiful, or more excited in my life.

By the time we got to the center of the compound where the ceremony would take place, the men had everything set up.

They'd made an alter out of twisted tree branches, twigs and flowers. It was beautiful. My mates were all there, dressed in black silk shirts and dark jeans and boots.

My heart nearly burst wide open when I saw them, especially when I saw the looks in their eyes as they laid them on me.

The four of us stood in a circle and Clay, as the figure-head of the male alphas of the pack, spoke the words that Ridge had remembered from the mating ceremonies of his youth, bonding us all together, forever.

Once the formal ceremony was over, the changing would take place. Of course it was what I was most nervous about.

I'd be bitten, by Ridge, since he was the most dominant.

They said within minutes I would begin the trans-formation.

Courtney told me it would hurt just a little the first few times, but once my body adjusted, there would be days when I ached for it. Ridge stepped up close to me and I tipped my head back as he lowered his. I was surprised when he grabbed my face with both hands and instead of just going in for the bite, he kissed me. It was a long, hot, deep kiss and when I was breathless and my head was spinning, he slid his hot lips down my jawline to my neck. When I felt him there, I closed my eyes tighter and braced myself for the bite. I felt a small prick at first and then a shot of adrenaline, not pain, as he sunk his teeth into me.

The adrenaline turned into the most incredible feeling of lust and desire that I'd ever experienced. I forgot we were being watched by the entire pack and I honestly wanted to take him right then and there. It was only when I felt him let go of me and take a step back that I opened my eyes.

Ridge was looking at me with the same kind of lust I was feeling, and strangely, I was drawn to the slight trickle of blood on his bottom lip...my blood. I took a step forward and like a wild animal, I licked at it, until I felt my body begin to change.

My muscles seemed to be stretching and my bones shifting. A shot of excruciating pain ran through me, and then just like that it was gone. I don't know how long any of it lasted, but suddenly my body was still once more and I was warm and comfortable. I looked around and every eye was on me, and Grayson was the first one to speak.

"Cheyenne, you're gorgeous." A mirror was brought around by two of the pack members and I felt chills all over my body when I got a look at myself. I was as black as night and my fur shone like gloss. My own eyes looked out at me; they were the only things I recognized. It was surreal, especially when I was suddenly surrounded by all three of my mates, my wolves at that moment. Another surge of adrenaline hit me and I instinctively knew I was ready for "the run."

Ridge took off first and the three of us followed. He led us through the woods and across the beach and back up into the hills. We ran across the loamy earth, our paws pounding into the dirt and foliage there and through bushes and over logs. It was the most freeing feeling I'd ever experienced and I knew Courtney was right, and soon I would crave that feeling, over and over again.

Ridge led us to a clearing once the four of us were spent from running. A little brook ran through it, fed by the waterfalls higher up on the hill. We drank from it until we were satiated and then I watched Ridge transform back into the incredibly hot man I fell in love with.

Chase and Gray shifted simultaneously and then it was my turn, but it dawned on me, I didn't know how.

Ridge came over and ran his hand down my fur, the way I'd touched Gray so many times. "Just close your eyes baby, and see yourself."

I did that, and it took me a few tries, but once again I felt the sting and burn as things stretched, shrank and rearranged. I only knew my transformation was complete when I saw the faces of my mates as they looked at me, completely naked on the grass in front of them.

"Jesus," Chase whispered, "You're even more beautiful than I imagined."

Ridge was nodding. "Me too."

Grayson grinned and said, "I've seen her already."

He got a push on the shoulder from Ridge that nearly knocked him over, and then Ridge came toward me first. I could feel lust rolling off of him like a heat wave, and colliding with mine.

My breaths sped up and my heart was racing. I was both nervous and more excited than I'd ever been, all at the same time.

Suddenly Ridge bent down and scooped me up into his strong arms. He carried me over to a spot that I hadn't noticed before. It was set up for us, a pile of comfortable looking blankets and a basket of fruit, and a bottle of champagne.

Candles surrounded the area in the dirt and as Ridge lay me down on the blankets, Grayson lit the candles.

I looked around at all three of them then, surrounding me and smelling strongly of desire.

Had I not been able to smell it, I would have seen it. Their erections were all big, hard and even throbbing.

Ridge touched me first, using his big hands to feel me, from my shoulders, and down my arms, and then back up to my chest where he kneaded and massaged my full breasts.

He leaned down and kissed each one of my nipples. I gasped, both at the feel of his lips on the engorged nubs and the idea of two other men watching.

Ridge didn't seem to even remember they were there, or care. His hands moved down to my hips where he slid them under my body and groped hungrily at my butt cheeks.

Then suddenly my gasp turned into a loud moan as he ran his big fingers down between my legs, wetting them with all of the excitement that had poured out of me, before sliding two up them up into my aching, tight pussy. I heard him gasp as my muscles contracted around his fingers and while he moved them in and out of me, he leaned down for a kiss. I kissed him like I was starving, moving my hips in time with his fingers, needing more.

Ridge obliged by sliding another finger inside. Now he was fucking me with three fingers as I pressed my heels into the ground and brought my butt up, so I was riding his hand like a wild animal. I'd lost sight of my other two mates, but that didn't last long.

I smelled Grayson first.

While Ridge was still pressing his fingers in and out of me, Grayson slid his hot mouth over one of my nipples and began to suckle at my breast. I cried out and put my hand in his hair, tangling my fingers through it and pressing him harder into my chest.

It wasn't long before Chase wanted in on the action. Ridge had pulled back and I could tell he was getting in position to slide his big cock into me, and just as I felt the tip of it press against my lips, I felt Chase's own throbbing member slide against my cheek. I didn't even think twice about it. I turned my head and opened my lips, engulfing as much of him as I could reach.

Chase let out a sexy groan just as Ridge slid into my sopping wet pussy. As I opened up for him, my muscles spasmed around his hot cock.

Chase had most of his in my mouth and I was sucking and licking at it wildly while Ridge began to move in and out of me, faster and harder with each stroke. Our hips began to meet each time and the harder he fucked me, the wilder I got with my mouth on Chase's cock and the harder Grayson bit and sucked at my breasts.

It was the most wild, incredible thing that had ever happened to me, and like when I first found out they were shifters, my brain was even still having a hard time believing it was real.

Ridge reached down and took the breast that Grayson wasn't sucking in his hand. He twisted and pulled and pinched at my nipple while not missing a beat plunging in and out of me. I rocked my hips and sucked harder on Chase's cock.

I could feel Chase swelling, he was getting ready to go any second. I brought one of my hands up and took hold of his soft sac. It was full and when I touched it, he groaned even louder than before and said my name.

I gave his balls a little squeeze with my fingers and Chase and Ridge both, erupted simultaneously. I was filled with the hot seed of two of my lovers at the same time from either end, and incredibly...I loved it.

Even more incredible was as soon as Ridge pulled out of me, Grayson was there, ready to move in, and I wanted it. I needed more.

Maybe this wolf thing had increased my libido, or the idea of having all three of them, or the fact that I hadn't had sex in over a year. Maybe it was all three combined, but whatever it was, I opened my legs and reached for Grayson's hard erection and guided him into my pussy like I hadn't just been fucked.

He moaned as he slid inside of me, pushing until I couldn't take any more and then he just held himself there for a few seconds, not moving, just reveling in the feel of us being joined. I felt a mouth clasp around one of my breasts and then the other. I opened my eyes to see that Ridge and Chase had both taken one and just as Grayson began to move his hips, they began to suck.

Ridge was rougher using the sides of his teeth to scrape against my nipple.

Chase suckled softly and used his tongue a lot. It was incredibly erotic to have both of my breasts pleasured at once, by two such different men.

Meanwhile, Grayson was proving that although he was young, he knew what he was doing when it came to making a woman feel good. He did this circle thing with his hips every time he was all the way inside of me, that caused his cock to slide over my G-spot and made me want to scream. I let it build up until I felt him swell and harden even more inside of me, and I knew he was reaching his peak. Then I dug my fingernails into the flesh of his arms, arched my back and let my own orgasm slam into me like a load of bricks.

Grayson cried out as he began to empty, mixing with Ridge's seed already inside of me. That thought turned me on even more and I flexed my pussy muscles and milked him until I'd drained him of every drop.

Finally I didn't have the energy to hold myself up any longer and I collapsed back down onto the blanket. I felt Grayson collapse down next to me, and I cuddled my body up to his and stroked his hair as Chase's lips met mine. Ridge continued to stroke his hands over my body, like he just couldn't get enough.

The four of us mated many times that night, in many different ways. It was like we had all taken lessons and were now performing a perfectly choreographed dance. It was like Ridge had said from the very beginning, we belonged together. Back then he hadn't been talking about Chase and Gray too, but I could see and feel that he realized it, the way that I did...we completed each other.

We fed each other fruit and they drank champagne from my belly button.

By the time the sun came up the next morning we were spent, sore and sticky. We bathed in the creek and then shifted back to our wolves and went for a long run before returning to the compound to begin our lives together. I couldn't wait...I was finally happy and I knew in my heart that there was so much more happiness yet to come.

THANK you so much for reading **Claimed by the Pack**! If you're looking for another steamy reverse harem read, check out **Desired by Four** *or see a listing of my complete works at the end of this book.*

Falling in love isn't supposed to be literal.

Except if you're a witch who's cast a soulmate spell… Turns out love magic isn't the kind you dabble with…

First there's Dixon with his sweet midwestern twang. Then there's action-hero-hot Mateo, who literally swooped in and saved my life… plus his three insanely handsome brothers. The universe definitely heard my call and it's raining men alright.

Seems that, *controlling* the magnetic attraction is where it gets tricky, especially if you happened to call upon a magical being, intent on killing you and stealing your power. Whoops.

Fortunately I've got four hot shifter protectors because I'm gonna need 'em.

books2read.com/desiredbyfour

Or Keep Reading for a Sneak Peek!

DESIRED BY FOUR

JADE ALTERS

ELLIE

I threw out the last of the takeout from my early dinner, carefully wiping the crumbs on my desk into the little trash bin underneath. Logging off my computer, I grabbed my keys and my phone, shouldered my purse, and took one last look around my office before turning out the light and locking up behind me. I was the last one out at Wilhelm Realty, as I was most evenings. I tended to work late and I'd been teased before for my, perhaps, excessive thoroughness. But I'd also made Realtor of the Month five times and that had come with some nice bonuses. I stopped by the restroom in the lobby on the way out to fix my hair, rinse out my mouth, and apply some lip balm.

There's not much out of place about me at any given time.

Unfastening my sleek, dark ponytail worn low on my head, I combed out my hair before fastening it neatly again. I checked my teeth again for any crumbs. I took the well-loved tube of Pomegranate Burt's Bees from my purse and put on a couple of good coats. It was spring in Boulder, Colorado, and the cool, dry air played havoc with my lips and skin. As usual, I'd applied some light make up that morning; BB cream, neutral shadow, mascara, and my balm. But I wasn't going anywhere now that required makeup and didn't refresh before I left the restroom, turned out the floor lights, and stepped out into the crisp and breezy April night to lock the front doors of the office on Pearl Street behind me.

"Woo!" A cold gust of wind made me shiver and I cinched my coat a little more snugly around me as I crossed Pearl, and headed toward the parking structure. I nodded hello at the gate guy who always made a point of asking me about Indiana, my Welsh Corgi. When I pulled my blue Accord out of the lot, I turned left instead of right. For once I wouldn't be going straight home or to a happy hour with the girls, or to another disappointing date. No, tonight I was finally taking action in order to avoid more of those disappointing dates. This had been a long time coming, but as I navigated the lightly populated streets of downtown Boulder on a Thursday night and headed towards Settler's Park, it felt like the right decision.

"Do I want caffeine?" I murmured, chewing on my lip as I eyed the Starbucks two blocks up ahead. I would be out a bit late and needed to stay alert, which surely justified buying myself chai latte. Even at seven o'clock at night. Giving in, I circled the block and found street parking.

The sun wasn't fully set yet anyway, and it would need to be fully dark out for my purposes. I hung around for a few minutes at Starbucks, sipping my drink, and playing around on Instagram while listening to music. When it was good and dark, I headed back out and made my way down Pearl and straight into Settler's Park. I slowed down, humming along to Stevie Nicks, as I carefully turned into the winding road up into the woods. It was a little bit eerie out in the park this late but then that was sort of the point, I supposed. And it wasn't as if I was actually scared. I can handle myself pretty well generally.

Pulling over to park where the woods where things were almost dangerously dark and completely deserted, I pictured how I would look to somebody passing by; a woman alone in the woods at night. It probably looked like I was about to bury a body. I tittered at myself just thinking about it. Grabbing my sneakers from the backseat, I switched into them from my heels. In the trunk, I found two reusable grocery bags with all my supplies. I flicked on the safety flashlight on my keychain and checked just one more time to make sure I had everything. Satisfied, I took a breath, shut the trunk, and headed into the woods.

Tonight, things were finally going to change. I was taking my future back into my own hands.

I hated dating. Or I guess I should say, I hated how dating usually went. I tried for years and it never got any easier. I'd constructed carefully thought out dating profiles, written to show me in the best light while remaining authentic with my best face on display. It was always the same; an onslaught of guys who just wanted sex, a whole bunch of guys who ostensibly wanted to go on a date but were completely unappealing, and then maybe two guys who seemed like they might not be nightmares. Then I'd go out with the non-nightmares and there was just no...spark. The last time I'd felt anything like a spark was with an insurance examiner named David and the relationship had lasted three months before I'd realized I'd been working really hard to make myself feel a spark and I was exhausted. It's amazing what you can talk yourself into sometimes.

The last date I'd gone on was with some wine buyer for a tasting bar in town. I admit, I was sucked in because he'd been very attractive. Then I went out with him and he had nothing to say. As in, he didn't ask me any questions and he didn't offer up any information. He seemed to be happy with sharing complete silence during nearly the entire date and while I think being able to share silence once in a while with someone is a good sign that you're comfortable with them, it was the strangest date I'd ever been on and I'd ghosted him when he texted afterward. I don't need constant clever conversation, but I do need to be able to talk to somebody for Pete's sake.

Suddenly, I'd looked around and realized that dating was kind of an insane proposition. You find some random person you think is physically attractive and who you don't immediately dislike and spend a few hours together with the expectation of romantic interest. No pressure there!

So, I'd decided to opt out. No more dating for me. I'd been told to be patient again and again but after so many years of being patient, it seemed like a new strategy was in order. Because the truth was, I *wanted* a partner. I'd built myself a nice career, I had friends and family. I considered myself generally pretty autonomous. But I couldn't lie to myself either. I wanted passionate love. People had never thought of me as romantic. I'd always been down-to-business, practical, no-nonsense. Those traits describe me well. But that didn't mean I didn't want to be swept off my feet or to feel I was the center of somebody's world and to make them the center of mine. It didn't mean I didn't want to wake up beside a lover and feel the warm delight of them wrapping me in their arms.

So, new strategy. And since I happened to be a pretty well-trained witch, I figured magic was the way to shortcut dating. I don't often use magic. It's something that I've always thought I could take or leave and I'd never been deeply involved in the magical world. It runs in the family. My mother was a witch and she raised me and my sister in the craft. Our line goes back centuries. It's something I have respect for and I'm proud of the legacy, but I'd never wanted to center my life around it. Every once in a while though, it did come in handy. I'd put a few spells on houses I was trying to sell before and gotten some good results out of it. I once hexed the postal carrier because he kept leaving mail in the mud. He was chased by wasps for three blocks. To be fair, I *had* warned him.

My new strategy to 'dating' was a three-hundred-year-old spell that had commonly and traditionally been used to find women husbands back when that had been a matter of survival. I'd tweaked it a little bit. There were other similar spells but this one seemed to catch the best results from everything I'd read. Yet it was also a little too focused on *just* catching the husband. But I didn't want to just catch a husband. I wanted a soulmate, a great love. This spell, as I'd redesigned it, worked on the assumption that my guy, my great love, was out there somewhere. All I had to do was find him. It was a matter of fate.

I kept my little safety flashlight on and traipsed down a narrow trail through the woods. There was a particular spot that faced the moon and had a nice big boulder that I thought would be good for brewing. A boulder is usually good for brewing. There's often just enough crystallization going on to absorb the spell and throw it back on you, you just have to be careful you're not brewing around some volatile crystal that could seriously mess you up. But an igneous rock is generally safe.

I whistled to myself as I set out a blanket and set down my cauldron. The cauldron was my mother's. She'd passed it down to me before retiring to Florida with my dad. My younger sister got our grandmother's cauldron. We also have our own. Every decently raised witch gets their own cauldron around the age of twelve. But I liked to use my mother's for luck.

I set out my mini-lantern, flicked it on, and went to work. Some of the ingredients had been difficult to find. It had been a little while since I'd tried my hand at spell casting. This one called for aged blood. I'd cut my arm months before and let it sit in a jar out of sight just in case of prying guests.

I muttered to myself as I mixed the base; sulphur, sand from my home, feathers from a blessed bird… I burned sage and recited an old protection spell to keep the area safe while I was working. I lit a fire under the cauldron and brought up the spell on my iPhone. I began to recite the two paragraph spell, watching the position of the clouds around the moon carefully. This was an important night for the spell. The moon was waning but the sky was mainly clear. The moon couldn't be covered while I enacted the spell, it had to 'see' me.

"Bring me my fated one," I said quietly, shuddering at a cold gust of wind. "Bring me my soulmate, gods. One fire of love. Tie me to my love and let the tether remain unbroken."

I poured in two jars full of goat's blood, then the bit of my own blood I'd saved, along with a pitcher of lavender milk. The cauldron roiled and the wind picked up. I could feel the power of the spell in my veins and it made my heart pound. That was a good sign and I knelt on the blanket, spouting the spell as I stirred the potion while it bubbled and foamed.

"Bring me my fated one," I said louder. My hair came unclasped from my ponytail and whipped around my face and the trees rustled so hard I was sure they were speaking to me. Too bad I didn't know how to speak tree. "Bring me my soulmate, gods! One fire of love!" The fire under the cauldron flamed up around the cauldron for a second, singing my blanket, and my heart leapt, but I stayed where I was even as the wind blew pine needles and dirt at my face. "Tie me to my love and let the tether remain unbroken!"

Smoke began to spiral up from the cauldron and I smiled, feeling the almost orgasmic power of a successful spell thrumming through me. I raised my hands over my head and closed my eyes, trusting the magic not to kill me.

"Bring me my fated one! Bring me my soulmate, gods! One fire of love! Tie me to my love and let the tether remain unbroken!"

When I could feel the power of the spell peaking, I grabbed the mug I'd brought with me, dunked it into the cauldron and drank up the cup full before I could think about how gross it would taste.

And it did taste pretty gross. But I held it down, still reciting the spell at full volume as the spiraling smoke rose up into the trees and formed a heart before fading into the wind.

It had definitely worked. And I felt a bit giddy with the assurance that soon I would be finding my one true love. As self-made and strong as I consider myself to be, I wanted someone to laugh with who could challenge me and support me as much as I would for them.

Now, I was going to get him. I just had to keep my eyes peeled for the signs.

I felt the slow release as the spell came down and began packing my things away. A potion once catalyzed by a spell is harmless so I dumped the cauldron out into the dirt before packing it in a garbage bag to clean later. Finally, I stood with my packed up tote bags and flashed my safety light around to make sure I hadn't littered or left anything behind and when I was satisfied, I hiked back to the car.

On the drive home, I felt better than I had in a long while. It was a satisfying sensation to know I'd taken my future in my own hands rather than leaving it to chance or some stupid dating app. I cranked up the radio, singing along to Steve Nicks' 'Sorcerer' which felt strangely prescient.

At home, Indiana did his little happy tap dance when I walked in the door and I fed him before changing into my pajamas and grabbing the last of the Mint Milanos, ready to settle in for whatever my friends were telling me to watch on Netflix.

For some reason, when I sat on my couch, I always sat on the right side, with Indiana curled up next to me. It was weird because I had a big couch. It was as if I were waiting for someone to come along and take their seat.

And soon now, somebody finally would.

The next morning, I woke up excited. I was singing 'Sorcerer' to myself as I scooped granola into my Greek yogurt, swinging my hips a little as I applied my BB cream. I hadn't felt so giddy and positive in ages and never for anything so legitimately exciting. I suppose it might be different for somebody who doesn't understand the true power of a well-cast spell. But I do. The only potential danger or risk is that your interpretation might be different than how magic will interpret your casting. It's sort of a 'Monkey's Paw' situation. But I was careful about such things and confident that I'd cast it so that I wouldn't be surprised by any weird twists. The spell was meant to find you someone you'd love who would love you back. I wasn't worried that I was going to get seduced by some evil wizard or something. Because I was pretty sure I wouldn't fall for an evil wizard. Magic, in my experience, was benevolent as long as your intentions were benevolent.

"Indiana, baby!" I sang out. Indiana came tap dancing over to the kitchen as I slipped in my second earring, and I squatted down to scratch him behind the ears before spooning the rest of a can of dog food into his bowl. "Be good, sweetie."

I found myself looking around for potential soulmates before I'd even left my building. It was a little ridiculous. My guy was out there somewhere and I'd know when I felt pulled towards him. That was what I had to keep my senses alerted to. I trusted the fates.

I tend to think of myself as an observant person when I'm walking around in the world. But I don't often size men up as I walked past them unless they were particularly striking. Now all of a sudden, every man was a possible love interest. I found myself judging every man I saw. The guy carrying a tray of coffee as he crossed the street in front of my car had nice hair and good taste in suits but he wore a sour look on his face so I dimly hoped it wasn't him. The guy who pulled up next to me in a Lexus, singing along to Journey and bobbing his head was cute, I decided. I wouldn't mind if it was him. The guy waiting by the entrance of the parking garage talked too loud on his blue tooth but he also had a pretty smile so that was a toss-up.

At work, I had a few phone calls from nervous sellers. Their houses were all in a particularly nice neighborhood and the market was hot, so they required a lot of personal attention and it kept me busy all morning and into lunch.

I kept waiting to feel the pull towards my inevitable soul-mate. At one point, I thought I was feeling it as Andy, one of my co-workers, hovered outside my office. Andy was cute in a nerdy sort of way, and he glanced over at me once before taking a call on his phone. But it turned out that 'pull' was just my stomach rumbling because I'd worked through my usual lunch hour.

At two, I finally grabbed my purse, intending to eat at the deli across the street and down a few blocks. My stroll was leisurely as I sized up man after man. I knew well enough it was pretty useless to accept or dismiss the very idea of dating a person just by judging them in less than a second and only based on their appearance at the moment. That was the whole modern dating thing I'd rejected in the first place. I'd been swiping left and right for a few years. I had to stop thinking in those terms now and leave it to the pull.

"Trust the fates," I muttered to myself as I walked into Lovebird's Deli. I got in line, intending to order my usual chicken Caesar sandwich. The guy in front of me glanced over his shoulder at me. He looked like a construction worker type in coveralls with the top pulled down and wrapped around his waist. He wore a white tank top that clung to his impressive and sweaty muscles. There was a little bit of dirt or dust, smudged here and there. His hair was sort of adorably tousled. He looked at me and the corner of his mouth turned up for the briefest moment before he turned back. He was sexy. I squinted and tried to sense some kind of pull within me.

No, nothing. Just low blood sugar.

I ordered my chicken Caesar and an iced tea and took my drink and my little number on its metal stand to a free table to wait for my lunch. The construction guy was sitting at the table just opposite me with some roast beef and he kept glancing over, his expression a combination of wonder and intrigue. I started to get excited. Maybe this was it. My food came and I found myself eating a little bit more carefully, trying to look appealing. But I don't think I needed to try much. The guy couldn't seem to keep his eyes off me. They were intense eyes too, a deep green that eventually fixed on me without straying.

I'm an attractive woman, conventionally speaking. It's not as if I get approached constantly but I don't generally want for male attention, and like most women, I'm annoyed by too much of it. But I couldn't remember ever having been focused on like this. It might have creeped me out a little bit usually, but now I had the fates on my side.

This must be it, I thought. The spell was bringing me my soulmate. One fire of love, no waiting. Summing up my nerve, I raised my eyes to meet his and did not blink. I tried to look as smoldering as he was. I decided to be bold and make a move. So, I got up and went to the condiment bar near his table. I took some napkins and a packet of sweetener for my iced tea that I didn't really need and as smoothly as I could manage, I slid my eyes over to him. He was sitting facing me and his gaze was fixed on me like I was the only person in the world. I met his eyes again and smiled just enough before going back to my table and sitting down.

A minute later he was coming to talk to me. My heart raced and my fingertips tingled as he slowly and deliberately made his way to my table. I wondered what he was like. Did he like documentaries like me? Was he a dog person? Was he a decent kisser?

"Hey," he said, running a hand through his hair as he paused by my table. I was done with my sandwich now and sat sipping my iced tea. I raised my eyes to him, hoping my makeup was in place. "I don't mean to bother you but I was sitting over there and… There's just something about you. I had to come over and talk to you. Is that alright?" His voice was gravelly like he'd just rolled out of bed, and there was a little twang to it. I pegged him for a Midwestern boy.

"Sure," I said, nodding. "Have a seat."

The midwestern guy sat and leaned forward on his elbows. His legs were kind of long and his knees bumped mine under the table. "I'm Dixon," he said, in that gravelly voice of his. He stuck out his hand and I shook it.

"Ellie," I said. "Crawford. Nice to meet you."

"Nice to meet you too, Ellie. I'm Dixon," he said. His eyelids lowered just a little bit. His biceps bulged a little as he shifted around. He smelled like soap and sweat as I breathed him in. Everything about him was sexy, including the smile now slowly crossing his face. I kept waiting to feel that pull towards him, compliments of the fates, but it wasn't really happening. I told myself to be patient. Maybe that stuff would come a little later. I had to trust in my own spell. Besides, talking to a sexy looking man like this one wasn't exactly a chore. "You having a good day, Ellie?"

"Pretty good day," I said, Feeling a little bit nervous, I crossed my arms, pinching my skin just a little bit. The guy was very attractive, sure, but I really hate looking flustered. "And you?"

"Getting better by the second," he said, grinning fully.

I licked my lips and sat up a little straighter. "So you just had to talk to me, huh?"

"That's right," Dixon said. His eyes skimmed over me and I felt just a little bit naked. "Never felt anything like it before. Just had to make sure you didn't get away before I spoke to you. Have you ever felt anything like that?"

"I don't think so," I said, sounding much too breathy. I cleared my throat, blushing a little. I felt ridiculous but then, it's not every day you meet your soulmate. And this could be the one. I downed the rest of my iced tea and dabbed my lips with the napkin, wishing I could calm myself down a bit.

"You have the most beautiful brown eyes I've ever seen," Dixon said, fixing his gaze on me again. "Looking right into me."

I blinked at him. From any other guy, it would just sound like a line. But coming from a possible soulmate, I felt flattered. "Oh," I said. "Thank you."

He must have read my reaction as hesitation because now he raised his hands in surrender and leaned back a little. "I know, I know," he said. "I'm coming on too strong. It's not as if we know anything about each other."

"No, I guess not," I said. "But I wouldn't mind knowing more."

"Is that a fact?" Dixon said, and his eyes twinkled so brightly, it was as if he'd plugged them in.

"That's a fact," I said, chuckling a little.

"So, what's your favorite movie?" Dixon said, leaning on his hand.

"Oh!" I laughed. "I have no idea. I hate picking favorites."

"Well, there you go," Dixon said. He chuckled warmly. "Now I know something about you. You hate picking favorites. I am intrigued. Ask me something."

"Are you allergic to dogs?" I said, genuinely on the edge of my seat to hear the answer.

Dixon reeled a little, his eyes big. "Oh God, no. That would be awful." He shrugged then, looking sheepish. "I don't have one myself. I work construction and they keep me pretty busy. But I love dogs. Do you have one?"

"Welsh Corgi," I said. "His name is Indiana."

Dixon snorted at that and smiled slyly. "Is that from *Indiana Jones and the Last Crusade*?" he asked. "As in, we-"

"Named the dog Indiana," I said, putting on my best Sean Connery. "I wouldn't say that's my favorite movie, but it's definitely up there. It was one of my favorites as a kid."

"A fine choice," Dixon said, nodding. "A fine choice. Listen, if you don't give me your number soon, I'm gonna have to beg for it. You don't want that, do you?"

"Hmm..." I tapped my chin, pretending to think about it.

Dixon clasped his hands as if in prayer and his brow furrowed like a sad puppy's. "Please?" He said. "Pretty please with sugar on top, Ellie Crawford?"

"Since you asked so nicely," I said, smirking just a little bit. I found a pen in my purse and wrote my number on a napkin, signing it with a flourish.

Dixon pocket the note, looking very proud of himself. "You know what, I think it's destiny we just met."

"Fate?" I said.

"Yeah," Dixon said. "Exactly." He took his phone from his pocket, grimacing when he saw the time, and he tapped the table. "Shoot, I'm late getting back."

"Yeah," I said, sighing. "I gotta get back too."

"What do you do?"

"Real estate agent," I said.

"Ah! I build em', you sell em." He reached out to shake my hand again. "Well, have a wonderful rest of your day, Ellie Crawford. I'll call you."

"See that you do," I said, hoping I sounded playful and cute. He grinned at that and kind nodded to himself, touching me on the shoulder before making his way out.

I finished up my lunch quickly and made my way back to the office on cloud nine. I felt so much better now that I'd met him and it was such a relief not to have to worry about him being a creep or having some terrible deal breaker of a flaw. He'd felt it! He'd felt the pull towards me that the spell had cast and even if he hadn't known what it was, it had worked on him.

As I waited at a stoplight, I wondered why *I* hadn't felt the pull. I'd kept searching for that sensation within me, something that would tell me that this was definitely the one and…nothing. I wondered if maybe the spell had been just a little bit flawed? Or maybe it was harder for me to absorb those effects since I was a witch? Traditionally, this spell would have been cast by a witch on to somebody else. Maybe I did need to give it a little while.

Oh well, I thought and shrugged to myself as I slipped my earbuds in and turned on some music.

Dixon had felt the pull toward me.

That was the important thing.

I still had a few minutes left of my lunch. I'd told Dixon I was in a rush too just to be agreeable and not seem too desperate. Which was pretty silly in hindsight. But now I took my time as I walked back to work.

I was about to cross a street when I gasped at the sudden and intense compulsion I had to turn left and walk to the pharmacy one block over. The urge was so strong that my palms were starting to sweat as I stood there on Pearl Street. I had a feeling that if I were to go anywhere other than the pharmacy right now, something dreadful would happen.

The longer I stood there, the worse I felt. Though I'm a pragmatic person, I tend to trust in magic and my own intuition. I follow hunches and I'm attentive to 'bad feelings'.

So, I turned left and headed toward the pharmacy. My skin felt too hot, even while the brisk air cooled it. Yet I immediately began to feel better as I walked. The sick sensation of coming dread if I failed to follow my instinct faded quickly.

But now I didn't know what I was supposed to do next. I wondered if this had something to do with Dixon.

I walked into the pharmacy, feeling hesitant.

Just then, my phone buzzed. I had a text message from the pharmacy that my prescription was ready.

Now, that was weird. Being raised a witch, I believed such strange coincidences were meaningful. I just wasn't sure of the meaning.

I'd had a bacterial infection a couple of months back and the doctor had prescribed ongoing antibiotics for a few months just in case. But I couldn't remember dropping off the slip. I must have, I thought. Perhaps I'd been too distracted by planning my spell and just forgotten that I'd done it. Or just as likely, maybe the doctor had ended up calling it in for me. He was only a few blocks away. Still, it was pretty strange that I'd had that gut feeling to walk to the pharmacy before getting the text. Fates didn't usually alert you to such mundane things as a prescription refill. There must be more to it, I thought.

I picked up my prescription and paid the few bucks after insurance but I had a strange feeling as I ambled out of there. I felt like there was something I was supposed to be doing, someone I was supposed to see.

I kept an eye out for Dixon. Maybe he was in trouble?

I was so busy worrying about whether my new soulmate was in danger and if the fates were trying to help me help him, that I forgot to pay attention to my own safety. I wasn't even aware of the light as I stepped off the curb and nearly got plowed down by a car.

But suddenly there was a strong arm, curving around my waist and yanking me back as smoothly as if it had been choreographed. My heart pounded as the car that would have plowed right into me sped by, and I stood there on the pavement, catching my breath.

"Are you alright?" The voice was low and smooth, but I didn't hear the question the first few times the stranger said it. I blinked at him, feeling horribly foolish. I was never so distracted or flaky.

"Yes," I said, smiling sheepishly. "Oh God, thank you so much. I don't know where my head was. I could have been killed."

"I'm certainly glad you weren't." The stranger shuddered a little. He was tall, a little taller than Dixon, and he had warm brown skin and jet black hair buzzed short in a way that suited his squarish face. He looked a little bit like an action hero and there was a subtle kind of charisma about him that made me want to lean in closer.

"Well..." I felt flustered suddenly, and not on my game at all like when I'd spoken to Dixon. "Thanks to you." My cheeks were burning. It was a little ridiculous. Though I supposed I was just embarrassed. And objectively speaking, the man was incredibly attractive. His features looked sculpted and long, thick eyelashes framed brown eyes that glittered warmly as he smiled.

"Only too happy to help," he said, waving a hand. "I'm Mateo. Mateo Marquez. If you plan to keep stepping off curbs into traffic, I'm going to have to keep an eye on you."

That made me laugh and I tucked my hair behind my ear. Dimly I thought of Dixon. Dixon. It was hard to remember Dixon as this man fixed his gaze on me.

"I'm Ellie," I said. We didn't end up shaking hands. Instead, we awkwardly stared at each other as if waiting for something to happen. Somebody brushed against me and that simple movement broke the spell. I laughed nervously and Mateo cleared his throat, his eyes flitted around. He seemed as off-kilter as I was.

"Alright," Mateo said, scratching his head and frowning. "I'm going to let you get back to it. Um...just be careful, please? I saved your life, that means you have to grant me that one wish."

I chuckled at that and nodded. "Will do. Thank you." I swallowed and our eyes met again. I felt pulled in, lost, welcomed... But Dixon... "Mateo," I said softly.

"Right," Mateo whispered and cleared his throat before seemed to come back to himself. He spun on his heel with one last nod and walked away.

I turned away from him. I felt short of breath as if I'd run a long way and I knew it didn't have anything to do with almost getting hit by a car.

I felt an inexplicable urge to look back at him that was so strong, I couldn't possibly deny it. When I looked back, Mateo was looking back at me from the end of the block. When our eyes met, he turned his head again. I blushed but simply turned away again and headed back to work.

I was confused and wondered if there was something more to the spell that I was missing. Dixon had definitely felt the pull. What he'd described had to be more than a coincidence.

I wondered if what I'd felt with the pharmacy and the man who'd saved me had just been a test. Very old fashioned spells used to have similar little tests of loyalty or will. I didn't think this one had, but maybe I'd missed it.

In any case, if it was a test to see if I was completely loyal to my new soulmate, I'd surely failed.

books2read.com/desiredbyfour

Warlock's Claim

Historical Paranormal Romance

Secrets of Storyville

A Countess Betrayed

A Harlot Betrothed

Epic World Building Academy Romance

The Broken Academy

Power of Fire

Power of Magic

Power of Blood

Pacts & Promises

Bonds

Reverse Harem Escapes – Great for a Quick Roll in the Hay with None of the Guilt

Fated Shifter Mates

Mated to the Pack

Mated to Team Shadow

Mated to the Pride

Taming Her Bears

Mated to the Clan

Protected by the Pack

Claimed by the Pack

The Descendants :

Desired by Four

Fate of Three

Shared by the Four

* 9 7 9 8 2 0 1 7 5 2 1 1 8 *